My Fated One

FATED MATES SERIES

NATALIE ARTHUR

My Fated One is part of the Fated Mates Series, but it includes characters from my Mancini Legacy series and Cimaruta MC Chicago Series. All my books are all stand alone with NO cheating and HEA.

Even though they are standalone, they are best enjoyed if read in order.

Acknowledgments

Danni, this journey is so crazy! Thank you for being here with me!

Jessica, you are summer and I am winter. Always.

JD, thank you for spending late nights with and making sure I listened even when I didn't want to. Love you.

Kristen, we can do this. Together.

Nicole, I'm forever grateful that you're in my life.

Carissa, thank you for everything you do.

Mary, Tammy and Gretchen, thank you for everything. For loving my books and supporting me.

Arthur, you've always supported me no matter how crazy my ideas are. I love you so much.

Mom, you've always been my biggest supporter and I don't know where I'd be without you.

Caoimhe-Lea, you drive me absolutely fucking crazy. But I wouldn't have it any other way. Love you.

Taye, and everyone I'm forgetting who has supported my crazy ideas and continue to be with me, thank you. I truly couldn't do this without all of you.

No part of this book or graphics were made
with AI.
HUMAN CREATION ONLY

My Fated One has NO cheating and a guaranteed
HEA. It's part of the Fated Mates Series. And is
connected to my Cimaruta MC Chicago and my
Mancini Legacy Series.

Check out my website for current news and trigger
warnings.
Mancini Legacy and Cimaruta MC family trees.
Nataliearthurbooks.com

Athanasiou
(Polar Bear shifters)

Zeus & Athena

Ares

Eros

Adonis

Apollo

Artemis

*Ares, Eros and Adonis are triplets
**Apollo and Artemis are twins

NIKOLAIDIS
(WHITE TIGER SHIFTERS)

Panagiotis & Stella

Georgios

Kostas

Calliope

*TRIPLETS

GIACOMO
CAITRÍONA
CELESTINO
ISABELLA
FRANCESCO
LUCIANA
MAEVE
RÓNÁN
SAOIRSE
GRAYSON
BASTIANINI
FAMILY

MANCINI FAMILY

Cimaruta MC

President - Giacomo 'Forza' Bastianini

Vice President - Celestino 'Giustizia' Bastianini

Sgt-At-Arms - Francesco 'Bestia' Bastianini

Treasurer - Luciana 'Fuoco' Bastianini

Secretary - Isabella 'Dolce' Bastianini

Historian - Caitríona 'Forte' Bastianini

Road Captain - Connor 'Azrael' Byrne

Chaplain - Brennan 'Raziel' Doyle

Enforcer - Liam 'Amante' Murphy

Enforcer - Valentino 'Ombra' Marconi

Enforcer - Romana 'Fantasma' Vietti

Enforcer - Mitchell 'Granchio' Harris

Enforcer - Hollis 'Cavallo' Taylor

Enforcer - Rónán 'Ghiaccio' O'Callaghan

Enforcer - Fintan 'Toro' O'Callaghan

Prospect - Anthony Grimes

Contents

My Fated One

Chapter One

Kostas

I can't imagine growing up in any other place than Kefalonia, Greece. It's an island to the west of mainland Greece. I grew up exploring our island with my brother, Georgios, who is five minutes older than me, and our younger sister, Calliope, who's five minutes younger than me. We live here with our parents, Panagiotis and Stella Nikolaidis.

Living here, we've been able to find all of the hidden treasures of the island. There are underground caverns to play and swim in and forests for us to shift and run. When we turned seven, our dad started training us to fight. We had so much energy, this was a way for us to learn discipline and get exercise. We also learned a few different styles of martial arts. By the time we were fifteen, Georgios and I were competing against other clan members. Calliope likes fighting, but she's not sure she wants to do it professionally.

The humans we grew up around spread rumors and stories about us, but didn't know anything for sure. It's not that shifter and human mating is forbidden, but it isn't a normal pairing. Most humans think shifters are a fantasy, one they're told as a bedtime story. Sometimes stories were created to scare the humans, to keep them out of the areas that we used to shift and run in. For the most part it's worked. There were the few who didn't listen and would see a tiger or two roaming around, but of course as soon as they're sighted, poof, they're gone.

All three of us went through our first change together. It happened when we turned ten. That first time was excruciating. I've never felt pain like that before or since. It felt like all the bones in my body were rearranging themselves, because well... they were. But after all that pain? I felt free, more free than I had ever felt. My tiger made me see things differently. The smells of the forest, the ocean breeze blowing through my fur, and the colors that surround me are so much more vibrant than when I'm in my human form.

Over half of the people who live here on the island are shifters, mostly tigers, like us. We're white tiger shifters. In our community, there are mostly orange tigers, some with stripes and some without. They look like Sumatran tigers. Then there's the few clans like us who are white tigers. There are also some that have thick stripes which make them look almost black in color. Each shifter family is their own clan. But the leaders of each family make up a council. It's a big council because of how many of us there are. Somehow it all works, and has for centuries. Each year, the council makes mating matches to keep the peace between the clans. They usually pick ten boys and ten girls and match them up. The year we turned fourteen, I was chosen. My dad made a deal with the leader of the Makros clan for me to marry his youngest daughter, Xenia. I'm not sure why Georgios wasn't chosen, I mean, he's older than me—shouldn't he get married first?

The deal was that we would be married when we turned eighteen. So that gave us four years to get to know each other and prepare. Their clan lived on the far west side of the island, and we lived on the far east side. We didn't know any of them.

From the minute we were paired, she hated me. I'm not sure why, but she did everything she could to avoid getting to know me. The only time she spent with me was when it was in front of our families because she had no choice, her dad was watching her. She would pretend to like me and talk to me. It was miserable, and the thought of spending the rest of my life with her made me angry. Shifters don't get divorced, cheat, or leave our mates. The only way out of a marriage is if one of us were to find our fated mate. That's the one mate that is our soulmate, the other half that was created just for us. It is rare to find your fated mate because there are so many shifters and we are scattered all over the world. There is one other way to get out of a marriage, but that requires one of us to die. And I don't plan on dying anytime soon.

Eight years ago, my dad met a man named Enea Mancini, the head of the Chicago mafia. They struck up a friendship when Enea and his family came here to Greece for a vacation. My dad talked to our council, and it was decided that he could tell Enea about shifters. They felt that it would benefit both families to share what we are. At first, he and his family didn't believe. Then they got to see us shift. After seeing what we are and watching us fight, Enea offered to sponsor us to fight in the United States when we were older. We had to be eighteen, though. So we've been planning ever since.

Our family has decided that after Xenia and I are married, we will move to the United States so that Georgios and I can compete in SMMA fights. The SMMA is the Shifting Mixed Martial Arts. The fights we'll be competing in are against other shifters from around the world. Humans and shifters share the SMMA world, but none of the humans know we're shifters. There are a few shifters on the board for the SMMA, and they made sure that there is a special section where only shifters fight each other. It wouldn't be fair if we fought humans. Even the smallest shifter has more strength than the biggest human.

In six months, I'm supposed to marry a girl I don't know and don't want to know. The last four years have shown me that Xenia isn't the woman I want to spend the rest of my long-ass life with. Not having many options, I'm not sure what I'm going to do.

Xenia's been staying with us for the last month and I dislike her more and more each day. She's tested my patience—and my tiger's patience, making me frustrated and angry. She still ignores me as much as she can. She's also disrespectful to my siblings. The only ones she's nice to are my parents, and that's because she's afraid of them. I hear her talking to her siblings and friends back home. I'm not sure if she thinks she's being careful, but as a shifter, she knows how well we hear and see things. So I'm guessing she just doesn't give a shit. She's always complaining how my parents hover too much and how she's not allowed to make friends. Which is complete bullshit. She doesn't want to make any friends here. All she wants to do is go back to her home. And I wish I could send her back.

"There's got to be a way for this marriage crap to go away. I don't want to marry her. She's fucking horrible," I growl at my brother as we spar together.

"I know. But you heard dad, there's nothing we can do to get you out of this."

"It's bullshit."

For the next two hours, we box, then switch to martial arts, taking some time to spar with Calliope too. Why couldn't I have been paired with someone that fit in with us? Or just been left to find my own mate? That would've been the perfect scenario. The ones that aren't put into arranged marriages are able to find love.

"Maybe we can head to the caverns today after we're done," Calliope says.

"That sounds good. It's hot today and a swim would be nice," I answer.

"Do you think we should invite Xenia?" She frowns.

"Ugh. Yeah, I guess we should. We can head home first, grab our shit, and see if she wants to come. She probably won't, but at least she can't say we didn't ask." I sigh.

After a few more hours of training, including shifting and going for a run, we're headed back home. My dad has worked hard to give us the life we live. We have a beautiful three-story house. It has six bedrooms and six and a half bathrooms. The backyard is spacious enough that we can play football in it, and we have a heated swimming pool that we use all-year-round. My dad had this house built to my mamá's specifications. It's her dream home, and I know she's sad that she has to leave it behind when we move to Chicago.

Artemis

There are around two hundred bear families that live on the island of Thasos. It's an old island with lots of history. Our family is one of the original twenty families. The bear clans have lived here for centuries. We came here from different areas of Greece and chose to settle as one clan. When Thasos was chosen, there weren't many humans, so it was easy to conceal that we were shifters. In recent years, the human population has grown, so we've had to be more careful of where and when we shift. Some families don't shift outside of their properties for fear of being seen. The council is thinking of petitioning for a piece of forestry that we can fence off and put a security system around. This would help make it safer for us to shift and run. Being a bear shifter, we're all pretty big, and we need to be able to run. When we don't shift for more than a week, it makes us very aggressive. And aggressive shifters are never a good thing.

Each of the original families have one person they've chosen to be on the council. Ours is my dad, Zeus Athanasiou. He took over from his dad, Orion, about fifteen years ago. The clan council makes the rules that we're all expected to follow. And we do follow...for the most part.

Being the youngest of five kids is easy. Being the youngest and the only girl? Now that's hard. There's always someone hovering over me and it's usually one of my brothers. We're part of a huge bear shifter clan, our numbers are in the thousands. Our family is one of the larger ones. I have four older brothers. Ares, Eros and Adonis are triplets. They're two years older than my twin brother Apollo and me. We were ten when we had our first shift. After seeing what our older brothers went through the year before, it helped Apollo and me prepare for our shift. When we shift, we shift into polar bears, so we're the rarer type of bear shifters in our clan. There are families that look like black bears and brown bears. There are even a few families that are striped and spotted.

I've never been one of those girls that liked frilly dresses or dolls. I wanted to do everything my older brothers were doing. But I did dream of meeting my fated mate. My one and only. In our clan, it's happened, but for most of us, it's a thing of legends. My parents and grandparents were lucky enough to meet theirs, which is probably why I held on so tightly to that dream. I've watched their stories play out all my life. When I met Aion Calimeris, I hoped that he was the one. Sadly, he's not my true mate, but it's okay. I've come to love him so much that I'm not sure it matters to me anymore. I can see living my life with him, and he says he feels the same way. We talk about our future all the time. How many cubs we want, the kind of house we will build, where we want to live.

Eight years ago, my dad met a man named Giacomo Bastianini. He's the president of the Cimaruta MC Chicago. We've heard of the Cimaruta. There's a chapter in Italy and one in Ireland. Our council allowed Giacomo and his family to witness our changes. They were sworn into secrecy for it, and so far, they've kept our secrets, making great allies of our clan. When Giacomo saw some of the guys fighting in human form, he was blown away. He said he'd love to sponsor fighters that want to compete in the SMMA circuit in America. There have been quite a few of our clan that has gone to America to fight, but my brothers are the ones that Giacomo wants. He and my dad have become close friends, and we have connected with his children too. They have twin boys and twin girls, and seeing as I don't have any sisters, I love that I'll get to hang out with Isabella and Luciana. They're six years older than Apollo and me. The times that we've spent together so far have been a blast.

Aion's family plans to come with us when we move to America. Aion has an older brother, Homer, and a younger sister, Phoebe. All of us were invited to participate in pre-fights to qualify for the SMMA in America. I'm not sure if I want to be a cage fighter. The best part is I can try it out, and then make up my mind. I don't have any set plans if I decide not to fight. Maybe I'll help my parents with my brothers' careers. So many decisions to make as you get older. Almost makes me wish I could just stay this age. My parents make the decisions, all I have to do is follow through.

Aion and I have been together for three years. He keeps telling me that when we turn eighteen, he's going to marry me. He's supposed to ask my dad for permission this weekend. I'm so nervous. I never know what my dad is going to do. I know he likes Aion, but I don't think he likes him enough to say yes. Because he and my mother are fated mates, I know he's holding out for my brothers and I to find ours. I know I love Aion, and I can see a future with him. But my dad makes me wonder about would happen if I met my fated mate. If meeting my fated mate is like how my grandparents and parents met each other? I wouldn't have a say in it. When you meet yours, the pull is so strong, there's no denying it. There have been others who were married or in relationships when they met their fated mate. I've seen them try to deny the pull, sometimes they were able to stay with their chosen mate. No matter how much I love Aion, it could happen to us. But the chances are slim, so I try not to think about it too much.

Apollo and I will be graduating in five months, and we turn eighteen two months after that. I'm hoping that Aion and I can be married before we leave for America. It would be great to start our new lives in America as a married couple. But if we can't, it'll be okay because we'll be there together.

Chapter Two

Kostas

"Whose car is that?" Georgios says as we park in the driveway. We each have a spot for our cars in the garage, but this unfamiliar car is blocking our garage door.

As we get out of the car, we can hear music blasting from inside the house. It's Xenia's crappy music. I recognize it because she plays it whenever my parents are out of the house.

"Maybe one of her friends or sisters came to visit?" Calliope asks.

I shrug my shoulders at her. "She never talks to

me, so I wouldn't know. Mamá and Dad didn't say anything about it."

We head inside the house where the music is almost deafening. Georgios and Calliope go to their rooms to get their stuff together. I follow the music towards her room and knock on her door. Her room is next to mine. I can hear other noises over the music. I'm not sure if something's wrong, and when I try to open the door, it's locked. So I kick it in. What I see next is something I never want to see again.

She's naked and riding a guy named Casper, who lives down the road. His clan moved from the United States and into our neighborhood about five years ago. Somehow, neither of them have heard me yet. So I whip out my phone and start recording. Xenia is screaming, "Yes! Fuck me!" while he's under her grunting like a pig. I get all of it on my phone. This is how I'm going to get out of marrying this girl. My parents will never accept her into our family now.

Georgios and Calliope are suddenly right beside me with their phones out too.

"Hey!" I yell as loud as I can.

What happens next is something that we still laugh about. Casper finally sees the three of us standing in the room, and he throws Xenia off of him. She lands on the floor, slamming into her radio on the way down, and it shuts off. He grabs his clothes and pushes us out of the way as he runs out of the room. We hear the front door open and slam shut. He never once looked at any of us.

"What?" Xenia says as she smirks at me, while standing there naked.

"What do you mean, 'what'?" I frown.

"Get the fuck out of my room. You've ruined my fucking day. In fact, you ruined my life the minute we were put together as mates," she spits out as she flashes her bear at me. Like I have any fucking say in who the council chooses.

I hold my tongue for now. If I say what I really want, I could screw up getting her out of my life. Calliope is still recording Xenia and her tantrum. What she doesn't realize is that Georgios has walked out of the room to call our parents. This is my ticket out of this arranged marriage. There are only two things that would make our council dissolve an arranged marriage. One is finding your fated mate. That one person that you're meant to be with—the other half of your soul. And the other? Cheating on your mate. The mate that was wronged is given the opportunity to reject the mate the council chose for them.

When my parents get home, Xenia is nowhere

to be found. If I had to take a guess, she's at Casper's house, probably finishing what we interrupted earlier. Don't get me wrong, I didn't think she was a virgin. But I did expect her to not fuck around when she moved in with us. I want to have fun too, but I've been holding back out of respect for her. Now I wish I hadn't.

"Where is Xenia?" I hear my mamá ask as she and my dad walk in the house.

I shrug my shoulders. "Right after Georgios called you, she got dressed and stormed out, screaming that I ruined her life."

"We got it all on video" Calliope adds.

My mamá sighs. "I had a feeling she was going to be a handful. Her mamá told me that she's their wild child. She had hoped this arranged marriage would help her to settle down."

I stare at my mamá. "Well, I knew from day one that she didn't want to be with me. She told me every time we hung out."

My dad sighs. "Can all three of you send me the videos so I can go to the council and get this marriage canceled? Unless you want to go through with it."

"Ew. No. I never wanted to be married to her."

My parents are laughing at me. Mean.

"Well, the council will most likely force Xenia

to marry Casper now. And they won't be allowed to wait. I wouldn't be surprised if her parents are summoned here as soon as the council sees the videos, and they're married before the weekend."

"She did just turn eighteen, and I think Casper is twenty," Georgios says.

My dad nods. "That's why I said they'll make it *now*. I'm glad you've been studying the rules. She doesn't have anything on you, right?"

"Nope. I haven't been with anyone since she moved here."

My mamá hugs me. "Thank you for following the rules."

I hug my mamá back.

Artemis

My family and I have been on vacation in Chicago, Illinois, for the last two weeks. We wanted to visit the Bastianinis and get all our plans in place before the move. We even found a house, and it's not far from the Bastianini's home. Every Christmas, our family takes a trip somewhere. Last year, we went to Galway, Ireland.

We're home a couple of days early because my

dad got called back for council matters. I was sad to leave Chicago, spending time with Isabella and Luciana was so much fun. This time, we got to meet their group of friends, and they're just as awesome as the twins. It makes this move easier knowing we'll have friends there.

The first thing I want to do is surprise Aion. He still thinks we're still in Chicago, and I even texted him so he doesn't suspect anything. He's going to be so surprised.

"I'm going to Aion's house," I say to everyone.

"Okay, please drive safe," my mamá responds.

"Or one of us can drive you there." Ares, my oldest brother, smiles.

"Um. Thanks...but no. I can drive myself."

My brothers laugh as they hug me.

"Ew. You're all sweaty." I laugh.

"Be back in a couple of hours. I'm not sure why the council needed me to cut our vacation short, but I want you all here when I get home," my dad says.

"Okay, Baba."

I grab my wallet, phone and keys. Since we're moving, we've started selling some of our things. We each had our own car, but now we all share two cars. It's not the best arrangement, but we make it work. I'm so excited to see Aion. I enjoy spending time with him. We've taken our physical relationship slowly, only kissing and heavy petting. I'm not ready to take the next step with him, and he's okay with waiting until we're both ready. I see his car as I pull into his driveway, so I park my car next to his and shut it off right away. I'm hoping he's watching TV or listening to music.

I get out of my car as quietly as I can, careful not to slam my door. I can hear music coming out of the house, so maybe he hasn't heard me yet. I go and get the hide-a-key that's inside a cute ceramic garden gnome next to the front door and let myself in. His parents know that I know where they keep it. Walking in, I can still hear the music. I think it's coming from Aion's bedroom. I sneak up the stairs and head to his door. It's weird because his door is closed, and he usually keeps it open when no one's home. I twist the handle and slowly open the door.

What I see is something I never thought I'd see. He's naked and slamming into my best friend, Daphne. They're lying sideways and facing the doorway, so I can see that both of them have their eyes closed. I get the full view of them fucking, and they still haven't seen me yet. I want to look away, but I can't.

"Fuck yes, baby," he growls at her.

"Aion, baby, harder," Daphne cries out.

I can't help the tears that fall as I watch them. Suddenly, I feel someone behind me.

"Aion! What the hell is going on?" his dad, Dimos, screams at him.

Aion and Daphne finally look towards the door. Daphne pulls away from him, covering her bits and tries to grab her clothes. Aion is staring at me. I don't know why I haven't left yet, but I feel like my feet are cemented to the floor.

"I'm so sorry, Artemis," Daphne whispers as she rushes past me. I hear Aion's mamá, Avra, asking Daphne why she's here and why she's naked.

"Get dressed, Aion," His dad snaps at him. Then he turns to me and hugs me. "I'm sorry, Artemis."

I nod as I wipe my tears, finally turning away from Aion. I make my way down the stairs to see his mamá and Daphne standing at the bottom. At least she's finally gotten her clothes on.

"Oh my god, Artemis," his mamá gasps as she comes over to me and pulls me in for a hug.

Daphne tries to make her way to the front door without anyone noticing her.

"Don't you move, Daphne," Aion's dad says,

coming down the stairs with Aion trailing behind him.

"I need to leave," I sniffle out to his mamá.

"Please, Artemis. I'm sorry," Aion says, coming over to me and touching my arm. His touch feels like fire, and I pull away.

I whip around to face him. "How long has this been going on?"

"This is the one and only time. I swear," he says.

"You're a liar, Aion," Daphne snaps at him, then turns to me. "We've been seeing each other for six months now. He said you think you're too good to have sex with him."

I feel like I've been punched in the gut. How could he do this to me? And all because I wouldn't do it? We'd talked about that, and I told him how I felt about it. He said he understood, and that he'd wait forever for me. Apparently, he didn't mean it. In fact, he didn't mean anything he's said to me. My bear is roaring at me to let her out. She wants to show Aion and Daphne exactly how she feels about them. And Daphne? We've been best friends since we were cubs. We met when we were six; her family had just moved to our area and joined our clan.

The look of disappointment on his parents'

faces tells me they had no idea this was going on. Well, that makes three of us.

"She's lying, baby. This was the first time, a moment of weakness because I missed you so much."

I laugh. "Are you kidding me? You missed me, so you fucked Daphne?"

He reaches out to touch me again. My bear lets out a snarl, and he jumps back.

"Don't you ever touch me again," I growl at him. My bear peeks out, making him take another step back. She wants to tear him apart, and it's taking all of my willpower to keep my change from happening. My body is starting to vibrate, and I need to get out of here before an angry seven-foot polar bear comes out. I struggle to get to the front door, telling my bear that she has to control herself. But she doesn't understand why. We were wronged by our chosen mate and our best friend, and she thinks they should both die.

"Will you be okay to drive home?" Avra asks me as she hugs me.

I wipe the errant tears that keep falling and nod, I'm not sure I trust my voice to talk.

"Please have your mamá call me when you get home," she says softly to me.

Daphne tries to sneak out the door.

"You were told not to move, Daphne." Avra growls.

"Sorry," Daphne whispers.

Aion's brother, Homer, and sister, Phoebe, come through the front door before I can make my escape.

"Hi!" Phoebe smiles as she gives me a hug.

I hug her back, trying to hide my tears. "I'm sorry, but I have to go. I'll talk to you soon."

"Whoa, what's going on?" she asks as she looks at everyone, then back at me.

"We'll explain later. Please don't forget to have your mamá call me," Avra says, hugging me again.

I leave before more tears can make their way down my face. When I get to my car, I can't get myself to start it and leave. How could he do this to me? Three years and it all comes down to the fact that I'm not ready to have sex with him?

I sit in my car for a few minutes before finally taking a deep breath and heading home. When I walk into the house, I smell fresh bread and hear my mamá in the kitchen. I head straight for her and fall into her arms.

"What's wrong, baby?" she asks.

I start sobbing as she holds me.

"Did something happen between you and Aion?" she asks softly.

I nod and finally wipe my tears. "I found him having sex with Daphne in his room. His mamá wants you to call her."

I can hear her bear growling as she listens to me. "Your dad will be home soon and we will take care of it. Aion won't get away with this."

My brothers choose that exact moment to walk into the kitchen.

"What did Aion do?" Ares asks.

"He cheated on your sister with Daphne."

"He's dead," Apollo snarls.

"Wait till dad hears about this." Adonis frowns. "Who the fuck does he think he is?"

All of my brothers come over and wrap their arms around me.

"Can't. Breathe." I gasp as I hear our mamá chuckle.

"You cannot go back to him. I don't care how much he begs," Eros says to me.

"I won't. I don't care what he says. I'm done with him."

My dad came home right when my mamá decided to call Avra. She tried to tell my mamá that it was a stupid mistake that Aion made. That they would make sure he'd never do it again. Before my mamá could answer her, my dad took the phone and informed Avra that her son will never come near me again. We could hear her trying to get him to listen to her and let them fix this. But there's no fixing what Aion broke. There's no coming back from cheating. And that's what my dad told her.

Chapter Three

<u>Seven Months later</u>

Artemis

Today, Apollo and I turn eighteen. And in two weeks, we'll be leaving to start our new lives in Chicago. Part of me is scared, but the other part is excited. Seven months ago, I thought I would be starting this new chapter with my family and Aion. But not after I caught him with Daphne. What happened after was a huge deal, and I haven't seen or talked to him since. He still calls and comes to the house, trying to get me to talk to him. But that will never happen.

"Artemis! Come on! Open the door and talk to me!" Aion yells from outside.

"That boy needs to stop." My mamá frowns. "I've talked to Dimos and Avra about this, and they said they would make sure he cut it out."

"Apparently he's not listening." I sigh. "Maybe I should just talk to him and tell him to his face that it's over."

"Fuck that," Eros snarls. "That asshole doesn't deserve another second of your time."

"But it might make him stop. And that's all I want. You can come outside with me."

"Fine. Let's get this over with."

"We're all going with you," Ares adds.

"That's fine."

We head to the front door and walk outside. Aion comes running up and tries to hug me. All four of my brothers step in front of me.

"You don't touch Artemis," Ares says.

"Come on, Ares. I made a mistake, and I'm sorry. I love your sister, and I want to spend my life with her."

I laugh from behind my sibling wall. No matter how hurt I am, I'll never let him see that. Seeing him with my best friend...that was the worst thing I could ever imagine.

"Are you seriously telling us that it was a

mistake? That the baby that Daphne is carrying isn't yours?" Apollo adds.

The color drains from Aion's face at the mention of Daphne's pregnancy. It's not a secret in our clan, and I don't know why he thinks I could ever look past that. She's eight months pregnant which means when I caught them and he said it was the first time? He was lying. If it was, she wouldn't be eight months along. As hard as I try, I still feel so betrayed by both of them.

"That baby isn't mine," he spits out.

"Are you kidding me?" I snap, still behind my sibling wall. "You rejected me, Aion. Plain and simple. You can't take that back."

"Baby, I swear it's not my cub. I never rejected you. You're the only one I want to have a family with."

"You rejected me the minute you stuck your dick in Daphne. So if this is all you came to say, we're done. We all know that cub she's carrying is yours. So don't try and tell me different."

"I'm telling you the truth, Artemis. It's not mine. Daphne even admitted it to me."

"You know what, Aion? Even if the cub isn't yours, I will never take you back. You did the one thing I told you I would never forgive. Now, you need to leave. Stop calling me. Stop coming to my house."

"Please. We can start over in Chicago. It'll be a new life, a new home. We can start again," he pleads. "Daphne won't be there. It'll be just us."

I try to block out the fact that his family's still moving to Chicago. In a perfect world, they would change their minds. But Homer, Aion and Phoebe were all invited to the tryouts too. Yay me.

"Let me say this again, Aion. I will never be with you, ever. I don't care if you think we can start over. It will never happen. You made the choice to fuck Daphne. You did that. We. Are. Done."

"Now leave," Eros demands.

My brothers move forward as one unit. They look like those viking shield walls that you see in movies. Just without the shields. It's actually pretty impressive to watch, and I can only imagine what it looks like from Aion's point of view.

"Come on, guys. You know I love your sister, she's my world." He looks a little pale as my brothers advance on him.

"Leave. Now. And don't come back. Oh, and when we get to Chicago? These rules still apply. You don't come near Artemis or talk to her," Apollo says to him.

"You'll see, that kid Daphne's carrying isn't

mine. Then you'll come back to me," Aion spouts out.

"If you really think that's the only reason I don't want to be with you, you're a bigger asshole than I thought," I retort.

Aion finally turns and gets into his car to leave. There's still a part of me that misses him and wishes he didn't do what he did. But there's no way for me to forgive him or Daphne.

"He's even more stupid than I originally thought." Eros laughs. "Does he really think the kid is the problem?"

"Right? Like I can forget seeing him fuck Daphne." I shake my head. I really need to try, though.

"We're going to go for a swim," Ares tells our parents.

"Okay, be safe and have fun." Mamá smiles as we all give her a hug and kiss.

"Should we go exploring? Or go to our spot?" Eros asks us.

"I just want to swim. I'd love to shift, but it's so hot." I laugh. "I don't think my bear wants to be out in this heat."

Everyone laughs as they agree with me.

"We could go to that cave we found. The one we had to swim about two miles to get to. Or take the boat. That way we could shift and get into the water," Apollo suggests.

"That sounds good. Can we borrow the boat?" Eros asks our dad.

"Yes. Just please be careful, and take the satellite phone just in case your phones don't work out there."

"Thank you, Baba. We'll be careful," I say as I hug him.

I'm going to miss our island—running in the forest with my brothers and friends, exploring and finding new caves to swim in. I know we'll be coming back to visit, but it's just not the same. Luciana Bastianini has said there are protected lands where we can shift and run. But shifting and swimming might be a little more challenging. There's Lake Michigan, but it's a wide open lake. I did see a few little islands in the lake that we might be able to play on.

Kostas

The council meeting my dad requested when I caught Xenia was scheduled for today. Caspers family left Greece a few weeks after I walked in on them. We will be officially informing the council that Xenia has rejected me as her mate. It should make me sad, being a rejected mate is never a happy thing. But...well...yay!

"The council is calling all the clans in for the meeting this afternoon," my dad says to everyone.

"Did you have to tell them what happened?" My mamá asks.

"No. I just requested an emergency meeting for later today. And they approved it."

"Do you think they'll still make me marry her?" I ask.

"No. Cheating is the number one reason they allow divorce and rejection of mates. But you will need to stand in front of everyone and tell the council what happened."

That's the one thing I hoped I wouldn't have to do. Stand up in front of all the clans and tell them that I was cheated on. That Xenia rejected me. Fuck. The best thing that's happening is that we're moving in two weeks. We're headed to Chicago and will be staying with the Mancini family until we see if my brother and I get accepted into the SMMA. If we get in, we'll be in Chicago for the foreseeable future. New adventures.

I'm getting more nervous now that it's time to go to the meeting.

"I'm sorry. I made a mistake," Xenia says from behind me. She wraps her arms around me.

I untangle myself and move away from her.

"Don't touch me. You made your choice, there's no going back from this." I turn to look at her.

She has tears falling. "I didn't mean to hurt you. I swear I didn't. It was a stupid mistake, and I will spend the rest of my life making it up to you. Please. Say you forgive me and ask your dad to cancel the council meeting."

I frown at her. I don't know why she's acting like this now. She's hated me from the day we were forced into this.

"What the hell are you talking about? You've never wanted to be with me. From the day we met, you told me this was the worst thing ever. And I have always agreed with you. I'm not going to take you back now. We're done. You rejected me the moment you let Casper stick his cock in you."

Xenia starts bawling, all-out screaming, bawling like a two year old having a tantrum.

"You have to forgive me! I didn't reject you! He forced me to have sex with him!" She's sobbing and screaming at the same time.

I can't help it, I start laughing. Suddenly, she stops.

"Why are you laughing? I'm telling you Casper took advantage of me!"

I pull my phone out and find the video I took of them. "This doesn't look like you're being forced. In fact, if anyone was being forced, it's probably Casper since he's under you."

Her face turns bright red. "You can't show anyone that!"

She tries to snatch my phone from me, which is laughable. She's five foot five, I stand six foot six. She can barely reach the top of my head, let alone my hands raised in the air. Her solution? She's now trying to climb me like I'm some sort of fucking tree.

"Get off me, you psycho," I snarl. My tiger growls, and she falls off me.

"The council will believe me, and they'll make you marry me."

"Keep thinking that, Xenia," I scoff, and walk away. No matter how much I wanted to be rid of her, it still hurt that she chose to do this to me. I'm not a bad guy. Of course, I didn't want to be married to her. She's horrible, but I don't feel like I deserved what she did.

Suddenly, something solid hits the back of my head. When I reach back and touch my head, it's wet. That bitch threw something at me, and when I look at my hand, there's a lot of blood.

"What the fuck is wrong with you, Xenia!" Calliope screams, running to me. She puts a cloth to my head and tells me to hold it there.

"Hold that to your head. I'm gonna go get Mamá," Calliope says as she runs off. Mamá's one of the clan doctors.

"What happened?" Mamá asks as she comes rushing in.

"That stupid bitch threw a vase at Kostas' head." Calliope points at Xenia.

Xenia is screaming at Calliope and calling her a liar. She looks like she's going to shift if she doesn't calm down.

"Get her out of the house. She's going to fucking shift," I say to them. I'm starting to feel a little woozy. I can feel Mamá poking around my wound.

"I need to get the little pieces out and clean this wound up. Stay still," she commands as I sigh and keep an eye on Xenia.

Georgios comes in with our dad, picks Xenia up and takes her outside right as she shifts. I can see them both out there with her trying to calm her down. She's snapping and snarling at them, and I'm pretty sure I saw her connect with my brother's arm. He looks really pissed. There's a huge roar from outside, and we see Dad's tiger towering over Xenia. She's still shifted, but in that second we turned, we saw her take a swipe at dad. Bad idea. My dad uses his alpha power to subdue her. Now she's cowering on the ground. I've felt my dad's alpha power, and it's not a fun feeling.

Each clan leader has power over their family. This makes it possible for them to keep us in line when it's needed. It's something all shifter families have. And since Xenia is supposed to be part of ours, my dad has this power over her too. Once we go to our council meeting, we will sever those ties with her, and she will go back to her family. I can't wait for her to be gone for good.

"Okay, your wound is clean. I can't put a bandage on it unless we shave that part of your head." My mamá sighs.

"Can we just leave it open? I like my hair." I frown.

My mamá chuckles. "Yes. We can leave it open, but it's fresh right now. I need to cover it up till it dries up a little."

I nod. "Thank you, Mamá."

My mamá, sister and I stand up and watch Georgios and Dad deal with Xenia. She's trying to get out from under Dad's alpha hold. She'll learn really fast that you can't disobey a true alpha. I remember when we were little, all three of us would try to get away with things. And for the most part, we just got scolded or grounded. But there were a few times that our baba used his alpha power on us. I still cringe thinking about how it felt.

Chapter Four

Kostas

Being a shifter in a city has huge challenges. The biggest one right now is the lack of places to shift and run. My tiger has been getting really antsy. He wants out, and I can't say I blame him. I love shifting and stretching my mind to let him take over. To explore as a tiger, you see and smell everything, and the city has a lot of smells. My brother and sister are feeling restless too. Plus, I don't think it would be good for a human to see a tiger roaming the streets of Chicago. They'd probably try to take us to the zoo. Our parents think we're anxious because we're still new to shifting. As shifters, we age differently from humans. So even our parents at the age of thirty-eight are still considered babies. The oldest of our pack back home just turned four hundred. This is also why we don't usually mate with humans. No one wants to watch the person they love die.

We've been staying with the Mancinis since moving to Chicago. But even before this, we already felt like they were family. Now that we're here and with them all the time, I can see how their mafia family is just as important to them as their blood family. Georgios, Calliope and I have been having a great time with the Mancini kids. There are four of them, two sets of twins—Sebastiano and Domenico, who are six years older than us, and Lorenzo and Giovanna, they're five years older than us.

Tonight we've been invited to a barbecue. From what Sebastiano says, it's basically a get-together with lots of food. I'm down for that. Shifters love food, and we need lots of it.

"Hello?" I answer when my phone chirps at me.

"Hey, Kostas! It's Domenico. Are you guys ready for the barbecue? We're coming to get you in like an hour."

"Hey! Yeah, we're all ready. Thank you again for inviting us."

"Of course! You're going to love the Bastianinis and their club. They're all really good people. Are your parents coming too?"

"They were planning on it, if that's okay."

"Definitely. We'll see you all soon."

Since moving to Chicago, we haven't run into any shifters, just a city full of humans. Shifters always know when there's other shifters around. Eventually, we will meet a lot of other shifters and not only tigers like us. There are tigers, wolves, jaguars—you name an animal, there's probably a shifter clan for it.

"They're here!" Mamá calls out as we hear a car park in the driveway.

"Hey! Come on in," we hear Dad say as he opens the door for the Mancinis.

We all head to the front door to say our hellos and get our hugs in. The biggest thing I've learned about the Mancini family is that they love to hug.

Doesn't matter what for, they'll hug you. They remind me of our family, we're huggers too.

"Ready to go?" Enea asks everyone.

"Ready!" we all say together.

"Wow, that was loud." My mamá chuckles.

We all climb into one of the four cars in the driveway. The drive to the Bastianini property is a nice one. I love driving through the city, it's so different from our island back home. There's always so many people walking around the city. The Bastianini family live on the edge, and the property they own is just as impressive as the Mancini's.

As we pile out of the cars, there's a sea of motorcycles and guys in vests with 'Cimaruta MC Chicago' on the back. All of the men are huge— some almost as big as we are.

Then the wind shifts, and I sniff the air. Shifters. There's shifters here and holy shit!

"You smell that?" Calliope whispers.

"Mate," I whisper back to her. I watch her eyes get as big as saucers.

"Are you sure?"

"Yes." I can feel her, my fated mate. My tiger is trying to get out so he can find her. I can't let him out, but it's getting harder to contain him. I've never felt this before, and I don't know how to stop it.

"You need to get away from all these people, I can feel you vibrating," Georgios says from behind me. "You need to calm down or you're going to shift."

I know my brother is right, but I can't get my body to move. I need to find her. I turn and see a group of people. There are four boys and a girl, and I know it's her. I can feel it in every fiber of my being. My mate. Before anyone can stop me, I make my way over to her.

Artemis

Chicago has been a lot of fun. We've been learning how to ride motorcycles from the Cimaruta MC. In seven days, we will have our trials for the SMMA. I still haven't decided if I want to fight or not. There aren't a lot of women that fight in the shifter world. Not professionally, anyway.

Today the club is having what they call a 'barbecue.' From what I gather, there's going to be a lot of people and food. I'm all for the food.

After seeing four black SUVs pull into the property gates, I feel this strange pull towards someone here. Holy shit, there's more shifters here. And one...

"You okay?" Apollo asks me quietly.

"Mate," I get out as I scan the newcomers.

"Holy fuck. Wait, what?" Eros says.

"I'm getting Dad and Mamá," Ares says as he runs off.

My eyes finally settle on a man. He doesn't look any older than me, and he's perfect. I can feel his eyes on me too, and I can't stop staring at him. My bear is roaring for me to let her out so she can show him what she is. But there's no way I can do that, too many humans around.

"Artemis, are you sure?" I hear my dad's voice, but it sounds like he's a thousand miles away.

"She's found him," Mamá says.

"Artemis!" my dad shouts at me.

I finally focus on my dad. He's right in front of me, and my brothers are surrounding us. I can feel the tension rolling off of them. They think I'm going to shift. And to be honest? I'm not sure I can keep my bear contained.

"I'm okay, Dad," I whisper. "He's here. My one."

Suddenly, there's tears streaming down my

face. I don't know where they came from, but I feel overwhelmed with the need to be near him. To hold him. Kiss him. My body and soul already know him.

Before I know it, he's standing in front of me. Everything fades around us, and it's just the two of us. It's like everyone else just disappears. My elusive fated mate, we found each other. I wrap my arms around him and feel his arms circle me. Home. He's my home. I breathe him in and lay my head on his chest. I can hear his heart beating faster and in sync with mine.

"I can't believe I found you," he whispers to me. His voice sends shivers throughout my body.

I look up into his eyes. They're the color of pine needles, mixed with gold flakes.

"My name is Kostas Nikolaidis."

"I'm Artemis Athanasiou."

My bear is preening for him as I stare at my mate. She wants out so she can meet his tiger.

"You're beautiful." He smiles. "My mate."

"My mate," I parrot him. "I've dreamed of you, but I never thought I'd find you."

Suddenly, I remember that there are other people around us. My parents...brothers...the club. I look around and see both our families surrounding us. They're all introducing themselves to each other. Our mothers are smiling, even our dads are happy. I can feel their emotions as we all stand there.

"Everyone's staring at us," Eros says quietly.

"We should explain what's going on to Enea and Giacomo," my dad says.

We head over to where Enea Mancini and Giacomo Bastianini are standing and talking. They keep glancing over to us. Because we have heightened hearing, we know that they're trying to figure out what's happened. They're also worried that our families are going to fight each other.

"Enea, Giacomo, we feel we need to talk to you about what just happened," my dad says.

"We were worried there might be bad blood between your families," Enea responds.

"Far from it. We've never met before, but in our culture, we have what we call 'fated mates.' They are mated pairs that our gods have put together. Most never find their fated mate, but some are lucky like Athena and me. Most have chosen mates," my dad explains.

"Like Stella and me, we are chosen mates," Panagiotis adds in.

"But aren't you different types of shifters?" Giacomo asks.

"In our world, the animal species doesn't matter, but yes, we Nikolaidis are tigers."

"And we are bears," Zeus says.

"What we are trying to explain is that our children are fated mates. Kostas and Artemis." My dad smiles.

I can feel the heat rising on my face as they all turn to look at Kostas and me. His arms tighten around me, and that makes my bear purr. Yes, bears purr. I can feel a rumble in Kostas' chest, and it makes me smile more. After everything that happened with Aion, I never dreamed I would find my mate. But here he is, and he is more beautiful than I ever imagined.

Everyone gets introduced and the smell coming from the barbecue is divine. The Cimaruta MC is a really great group of people. I've been watching them interact with each other and the Mancinis. It feels like they're all one big family, and I love that. They've also embraced us like we've been part of their family for years.

Only the core families know about us being shifters. Enea and Giacomo did ask our dads if it would be okay to share our secret with the members of the Cimaruta MC. They have what are called 'members' and 'prospects,' but the prospects aren't guaranteed to become members.

So our dad decided that the members can be told, but the prospects can't. We're coming back tomorrow, and we will share our secret with them then. It makes me a little nervous because what if they don't like that we're shifters? Or they could even become afraid of us like some of the humans back in Greece.

The only thing we can do is trust our dads. I know that they'd never put us in harm's way. It's still a little scary to share with humans.

Chapter Five

Artemis

Meeting Kostas last night was something out of a fairytale. My mate. My fated mate. Kostas is everything I could ever ask for in a mate. I hated for the night to end, but I know that I'll be seeing him today. Because today is the tryouts for SMMA. But seeing Kostas is more important to me right now.

"What does it feel like?" Apollo says from my doorway. He walks in and sits on my bed.

"What does what feel like?"

"Meeting your fated mate. Is it everything we thought it would be? Like how Dad and Mamá say it is?"

I nod. "It's the best feeling ever, when we looked at each other...it felt like my soul was whole. I knew in my heart and my bear knew too. She kept trying to take over the minute she smelled him."

"One day, I hope we're all as lucky as you."

"From your lips to the ears of the gods," Eros says.

I look up and see the rest of my brothers come into my room.

"You know, fated mate or not, he better not fuck with you. Because you're still our baby sister and no one hurts you," Ares says, sitting next to Apollo.

I chuckle. Sometimes being the youngest of five and the only girl makes me happy. When Aion hurt me, they were there to pick me up and help me through that pain. I didn't just lose Aion, I lost my best girlfriend too. Double whammy.

"What time are we leaving for the gym?" I ask.

"Mamá said thirty minutes. You gonna fight today?" Eros asks me.

"Yeah. At the barbecue last night, Calliope—Kostas' sister—said she was going to. So she made me promise to try out too. I think it'll be fun."

They all smile at me.

"You're a badass, Sis. You're gonna do great."

Ares grabs me in a headlock, and of course my face ends up in his armpit.

"Ewww." I laugh as he lets go.

I finish getting my clothes together, and we all head downstairs to get our gear. I hate that Aion will be there today too. His family still made the trip to Chicago because he and his siblings are on the same list as us for tryouts. But he doesn't matter anymore, now that I've found Kostas. No one will ever matter again besides him.

When we get to the gym, I'm anxious to see Kostas. My bear is so happy she won't stop hopping around. I told her she's acting like a rabbit, and she purred. Crazy bear.

We're the first ones to get to the gym, besides the Bastianinis. The Mancinis will be coming with Kostas' family. I need them to get here now.

"Good luck today," Luciana Bastianini says to me.

I smile at her. "Thank you. And thank you for the barbecue last night."

"I love that you found your mate. As humans, I think we have soulmates too."

I nod. "I believe you do too. Have you ever felt for another man the way you feel for Rónán?"

She shakes her head. "Nope. Never. From the

moment I met him, I just knew he was the one for me."

She has a dreamy look on her face as she tells me that. I love it. Shifters and humans are so similar; we love hard, and when we find our mates, we never look at anyone again.

"Artemis, can we talk?"

That's the last voice I want to hear today. I sigh.

"Are you okay?" Luciana asks as she frowns at Aion. "Do you know him? Holy shit. He's the one that cheated on you?"

"Yes, that's Aion," I respond to Luciana. "It's okay, I got this."

I turn to face Aion. "No. We can't talk, Aion. Please leave me alone."

Aion reaches out to touch my arm, and I pull back. I can't stand the idea of him touching me ever again.

"Come on, baby. I love you and I miss you. You know we belong together," he says, pleading with me.

"Walk away, Aion," my brother, Apollo, growls as he steps up next to me, along with our other brothers.

"Apollo. You know that Artemis and I are meant to be together. I just want the chance to prove to her that I'm sorry. I fucked up and it'll never happen again."

Apollo laughs. "She said no. Are you deaf? You'll never be welcome in our clan again."

Apollo is blocking me from seeing anything, and that's one downfall of being smaller than them. I feel Kostas as soon as he walks into the gym. The shitty part is he walks in while Aion is harassing me.

Kostas

All I can think about is seeing my Artemis. I can't wait to wrap my arms around her. In all the excitement last night, we forgot to exchange numbers. My siblings thought that was the funniest thing ever. They're assholes. I won't forget to get her number today.

I feel Artemis the instant I walk into the gym. I scan the area and see her frowning at some guy. I know he's a shifter, and her body language is saying she doesn't want him near her. Then I see him try to touch her. Fuck no. I make my way over to her, before I can get there, I watch her brothers make a wall in front of her. She comes out just as I get to her.

I take her in my arms.

"Are you okay?" I whisper.

"I am now." She responds by holding me tighter.

I look over at the guy who tried to touch her. He's glaring at us, and I want to rip his eyes out.

"Who's that?"

"He's my ex, and he's not important."

This woman is mine, and he's hurt her. I don't know how he hurt her, but I will find out. I watch him step around her brothers then turn and come towards us. He's shorter than me by at least four inches, and I've got probably fifty pounds on him. He growls at me, trying to let his bear intimidate me. That's laughable. I don't care what animal he is or who he was to her. I will tear him apart if he touches my mate again.

Artemis turns to face him. "You need to leave, Aion. I told you I don't want to talk to you ever again."

"Are you seriously choosing this tiger over me?" The way he says 'tiger' makes mine pull at me to let him out.

"Back the fuck off," I snarl at him.

Just as I'm about to square off with Aion, Artemis' dad appears with another man at his side.

"Aion, get out of here. You've caused enough problems," Zeus says.

"Don't screw up your only chance to fight," the other man adds.

"She's mine," he growls at both of them.

I laugh. "No. That's where you're wrong. She's mine."

"Fuck you," he spits out.

"You made your choice, Aion, and even if you hadn't, it would be over now anyway. Kostas is my fated mate." Artemis looks him straight in the eye. I love how strong she is.

"You're lying," he stutters, then stands up straighter. "Mate or not, I had you first. Don't you forget that." He stomps off like a child.

Artemis starts giggling as we all watch him.

"I'm so sorry, Zeus," the man I'm assuming is Aion's dad says.

Zeus nods at him. "Just keep him away from my Artemis."

"Is it true? Are they fated mates?" he asks.

"Yes."

"Wow. Congratulations to you and Athena. I will take care of Aion."

"Thank you," Zeus replies.

Aion's dad comes over to Artemis and me.

"I'm Deimos Calimeris, congratulations to you both on finding each other." He puts his hand out for me to shake it.

"Thank you," I say as I take his hand. He then gives Artemis a hug.

"I'm so sorry for what Aion did to you. I thought I raised him to be a good and honorable man. What he did is unacceptable. You deserve all the happiness finding your fated mate brings you."

"Thank you, Deimos," she says softly as she hugs him back.

We watch Zeus and Deimos walk back to where the other parents are.

"Are you okay?" I ask Artemis as I wrap my arms around her again.

She lays her head on my chest. "I am. You got here just in time."

Her words make my tiger purr. I can't wait to be able to shift with her, to see her bear and have our animals finally meet.

Fighting in the SMMA, we use our human form. This is because we can't control who comes to the fights, and our secret needs to be protected. I know it's petty, but I hope I get to fight Aion. I want to hurt him for whatever he did to my Artemis. We haven't been able to sit and talk yet, but we plan to tonight. Maybe we'll get lucky and Aion and his brother won't make the cut. Then maybe they'll go back to Greece.

Even knowing that Artemis is my fated mate, what I went through with Xenia has screwed me up. I plan to tell Artemis what happened and I hope she understands. I can see her warming up for her fight. Artemis and Calliope are fighting in the first rounds. My sister is fighting a girl named Phoebe, and Artemis' opponent is a girl named Marsha.

From what I can tell, Phoebe is Aion's sister, and he's standing about two feet from me. My tiger is pacing as we watch him. Because he's not watching his sister, he's watching my mate. That's going to stop. I start to walk over to him, but my brother steps in front of me.

"Don't engage that asshole," Georgios says quietly.

"How can I not? He's watching Artemis. It almost feels like he's stalking her."

We both keep an eye on Aion while watching Calliope get through her fight.

"Am I wrong?" I ask him.

"No. You're not wrong, but there's nothing we can do unless he touches her."

I growl softly. I don't like that idea. We cheer when Calliope wins. Next up is Artemis. Watching my mate fight makes my tiger so damn happy. Artemis is fierce and so focused. She's the mate I dreamed of.

It's finally my turn to fight and lucky me, I'm fighting Aion. I see Artemis walking over to me.

"Good luck." She smiles at me.

I embrace her, rubbing my nose along her neck and breathing her scent in.

"Thank you." I kiss her on the cheek. I want our first kiss to be between us. Not shared with everyone.

I head into the ring and am face to face with Aion.

"You know she's mine. She'll always be mine, you only think she's your fated mate. That's a fucking fairytale. Artemis' heart belongs to me."

My tiger is snarling at his words, and I want to remind him that we know the truth. I let Aion land the first hit. That always makes them think they're better than me. In fact, I think I'll let him get a few hits in.

"What, you don't know how to fight back? Fucking tigers. You're worthless," Aion snarls at me.

I unleash a series of jabs and add a well-timed uppercut. When the bell rings, Aion is swaying on his feet.

"Who's the worthless one now?" I quietly say to him, then turn to go to my corner. I sit on my stool and watch him. My tiger is chuffing—it's his way of laughing and it's making me want to laugh with him.

I hear Aion's dad ask him if he wants to stop, and he shakes his head no. The bell rings, and I stand up. Aion still looks shaky. I look at his dad, and he nods at me. Okay, if they think he can fight? I'll fight.

Again, I let him get a few hits in. Then, I use the same combo I used earlier. Aion is so unsteady that he doesn't see it coming, and he's out. I step back and wait for them to call it.

"Fuck you, Nikolaidis. You got lucky," Aion snarls at me as he slowly gets to his feet.

I shake my head at him and walk back to my family.

"Sore loser." Calliope laughs.

Georgios and I laugh. "He really is. I think he let his anger over losing Artemis cloud his abilities."

"Well, too bad for him." My sister smirks. "Everyone wants to go out for dinner."

I scan the area for Artemis. I can feel her, but I don't see her, and it's making me a little nervous. Not knowing where my mate is makes my tiger and me grouchy.

Chapter Six

Artemis

After watching Kostas fight, I head over to where my family is huddled up with the Mancinis. And here come the Bastianinis. Something's going on.

"There's been animal attacks in the city," Salvatore Mancini says quietly to both families. He's a police officer with the Chicago Police Department.

"What do you mean 'animal attack'? Like dog attacks?" my dad asks.

"No, not dogs. The claw and bite marks are bigger," Salvatore responds. "The coroner thinks either tiger, mountain lion, or something similar."

"When did the attacks start?" Enea asks.

"The first one was two years ago. At first it seemed like a freak occurrence, but it's been happening more in the last year. At first we thought it was a large dog or that maybe someone had some kind of exotic animal and it got loose."

"It sounds like there's a 'but' in there," Ares says.

Salvatore sighs. "There is. We tested the saliva collected, and it was a mix—human and animal. So either there's some sicko training animals to murder people, or—"

"Or it's a shifter," I finish his sentence as he nods, turning to look at me.

"How can we help?" my dad asks.

"I hope it doesn't, but if it happens again, would you be able to identify who or what it is responsible?" Salvatore asks.

"We can tell you if it's a shifter or human, but we won't be able to pinpoint who or what animal it is unless we already know them," Zeus responds.

"Right now, any help you can give me would be invaluable. It's not just my department, it's been happening in multiple counties and precincts. We have to figure it out before more people die."

"Just let us know when you need us. The only

thing is we track better in our animal form," Zeus says, and my dad nods in agreement.

"I'll make it work. I might have to share your shifter status with my partner Mac."

"'Partner'? Your husband?" Zeus asks.

Salvatore chuckles. "No, Mac is my partner at work. He's got a wife and five kids."

Everyone laughs.

"For shifters, 'partner' usually means the person you're with," my dad explains.

Salvatore smiles. "Cultural differences. By the way, congrats on all your fights."

We all thank him. "Do you ever fight in your animal form?"

"We do, but not around humans, unless they know what we are. We've been spotted occasionally, of course, but they usually think we're wild animals. It's harder to shift here in the city because all your tigers and bears are in zoos."

I smile as I feel arms circle around me. It's interesting finding my fated mate. I can always feel him with me, and I know when it's him touching me. I lean back against him as we listen to the results from all the fights. Both of our families won all our fights, so it's been a great day.

Turning around to look up at Kostas, I smile at him. He's so damn handsome. I stretch on my toes and kiss him softly. With everyone around, I can't kiss him the way I want to, but I couldn't wait any longer to feel his lips on mine.

My lips are still tingling even after we've stopped. Aion is the only other man I've kissed, and I can positively say it was nothing like kissing Kostas.

"I hope my siblings can find their fated mates because I want them all to experience what I feel for you," Kostas says softly as he nuzzles my neck.

I wrap my arms around his neck and nod. "Me too."

Knowing that I have to say goodbye to Kostas is giving me a lot of anxiety. My bear won't stop pacing; she's grumbling that we should never be away from our mate. I'm definitely not disagreeing with her.

"I'll keep all of you up to date on the attacks. They're happening more frequently now, and it's putting everyone on edge. Plus not knowing where the next attack will be doesn't help," Salvatore says, breaking through my happy bubble.

The only thing good thing is that Salvatore knows it's not any of us. None of us were here for the initial attacks, but there have been others since we got here, and the Nikolaidis' were here for some too. That might be a problem later, but we can't worry about it yet. Right now, we need to find out who's doing this. There have been shifters in the United States for a long time. I don't understand why they're attacking humans now. It's not like we need them to live, we're not vampires...

Kostas

These killings are making all of us nervous. Even though we're hoping it's a wild animal, we all know it's not. That piece of work needs to be caught and taken off the streets before they take us all down with them. Everyone in our families are worried. I've heard of rogue shifters. They have no clan, and they basically do whatever they want. Most go crazy because of the solitude, and they end up more animal than human. Because we are part human, we crave family and need to be around each other on a daily basis. That's why most clans consist of two or more families and they grow from there.

There are several reasons a shifter can go rogue, and sometimes it's not by choice. Some shifters choose to mate with humans. It's not normal, but it happens, and has been happening more often in recent years. My parents said when they were little, stories of shifters and humans were like fairy tales. And not the happy, fun kind. When shifters and humans mix, they have to decide if they're going to tell the kids about their shifter half. Some rogue shifters that were caught say they were abandoned right after their first shift. I can understand how scary that could be—being human and giving birth to a baby, then that baby turns ten and they shift into an animal? A lot of them freak out and abandon the kid. Sad? Hell yes, it's sad. But it's part of our reality. That kid could possibly be found by a clan and taken in. If it isn't? Chances are the kid will turn feral and eventually go rogue, killing other shifters and humans, maybe even animals. There's an organization that takes care of rogue shifters called the Cleaners. They hunt and capture them, then try to rehabilitate them. The reality is, if they can't be rehabilitated, they're put down. It's a sad situation for everyone, but it has to be done.

I hope that the attacks slow down. Otherwise, things are going to get really bad.

We will find out who qualified for the SMMA in a few days. If either Georgios or I don't get in, I don't know what we'll do as a family. And now that I've found Artemis, it makes things a little more complicated. Because I won't leave my mate, and our families have already started talking about our wedding. Which isn't unusual in our world—as soon as you find your mate, you get married.

We've only shared one kiss. I'm letting her take control when it comes to sex. Because I've wanted her from the moment I smelled her. It hasn't been easy holding her and not being able to kiss her and mark her. When the time does come, our mating bite is going to be spectacular.

"We should discuss what we will do if you don't make it into the SMMA," Mamá says to all of us.

"I can't leave Artemis," I blurt out.

"I know, son. We would never make you leave her, but as a family, we need to decide what to do.

Calliope, have you decided if you want to?" dad asks.

"I would like to, if they want me.."

Our dad nods. "Your mamá and I are proud of all of you. We'll support you in whatever you choose to do."

I've never doubted the love our parents have for us. They're our number one supporters.

"I think we're all going to get in. Each of us won our fights, and we're sponsored by a well-known family here in Chicago," Georgios says.

"I agree. I have a good feeling about all this," I reply.

Chapter Seven

Kostas

It's been a few weeks since Salvatore told us about the killings, and it's been quiet. I feel like by admitting that to myself I'm jinxing us. Because we all know something's coming, and it's making us very restless.

The Athanasiou clan is joining us on the Mancini property so that we can shift and run. The reason we're using the Mancini property and not the Bastianini's is because the Bastianini property has a few otter families living there. Sometimes when they look at us, you can see and feel the fear in their tiny faces. Other animals can tell that we're shifters, and we can feel their emotions.

We do have to be careful even on the Mancini property. Part of it is a campground, and it's almost the end of camping season, so there are quite a few people staying there right now. There are signs that say there are wild animals on the property so be careful, but you never know with humans.

It's always interesting to see other animals. They don't know what to make of us, and some will attack. But for the most part, they keep their distance and just watch.

This will be the first time Artemis and I will shift together. I can't wait to see her bear. She's told me about her, she's a polar bear. She sounds beautiful.

"You have the run of the property. We have about one thousand acres for you to have fun on. Just remember, there are campers and hikers still around. They've been warned about the wildlife, and we do have bears and mountain lions that wander in and out," Enea says to all of us.

"We really appreciate you letting us run on your property." Panagiotis smiles.

"Yeah, the otters at the Bastianini property keep looking at us like we're going to eat them. It's making me really sad." Calliope sighs. "I promise we don't eat other animals—well, let me rephrase that. We don't eat animals we run into while in our animal forms."

We all laugh. Calliope isn't wrong though, we don't kill others and eat them in our animal forms. Now in our human forms, meat is yummy. But the idea of killing another animal and eating it raw? Ew, no thank you.

"I'm so jealous of you," Giovanna Mancini-O'Reilly says. She's Enea's youngest and only daughter.

"Why?" Artemis laughs.

"Because. I want to shift into an animal! And you? You're a gorgeous polar bear! I want to turn into a polar bear!" Giovanna chuckles. "It's really cool."

Artemis chuckles. "Okay, yeah, it's pretty cool. But there's pain that goes with shifting."

Giovanna squints at her. "Pain to be a polar bear...bring it on."

Everyone laughs at their conversation. The pain associated with shifting can be pretty brutal. It's not like you snap your fingers and—poof!— you're shifted and can start running. Sometimes it can take a few moments to acclimate to being in a different form. But I wouldn't trade it for anything. The world changes when my tiger takes over. I'm still in control, but I let him lead me where he wants to go.

I walk over to Artemis and wrap my arms around her.

"I can't wait to see your bear. My tiger has been preening all morning waiting for you."

I love the blush that colors her cheeks, and I want to make it happen more often.

"My bear is anxious to meet your tiger too."

We all get into four-wheelers, we didn't have them back in Greece. They're a lot of fun and exploring back home with those would've been awesome, although I'm not sure how they would fare on our rocky terrain. It still would've been fun to try, though.

We're going to the campgrounds with the Mancinis and the Bastianinis so that they can show us what sections are best for our purposes. My tiger is making rumbly noises in anticipation, and it's making me laugh because he won't stop. He wants to run, but he also wants to be with Artemis.

"So this is the area that leads to the trails and into the forest. As you can see, there's still a ton of people around, but they're aware that there's animals here, so they should be okay. And there's so much acreage, you'll be fine. There's a couple of ponds if you want to swim too. You've got free rein of like nine hundred acres."

"We really appreciate this," my dad says.

"Is there a cabin available that we could use to store our clothes?" Zeus asks.

"Yes, we saved the most remote cabin for you. Just follow this map, and it'll lead you to it. It's a three bedroom, with two bathrooms."

"Thank you, we really appreciate this." My mamá smiles.

The cabin is far enough out that there's not many people around. In fact, I've only seen a couple hiking up the trail. We plan to shift in groups and then find each other later. We all want to explore and have fun. This will be the first shift that I won't be with my siblings the whole time. Back home in Greece, we never shifted without each other. Part of it was for security. The other part is we just like to be around each other. I'm sure we'll be in close proximity, though. They just want to give me and Artemis some privacy.

We decided that our parents would go first. I know it's an odd concept that we are naked in front of each other. But as shifters, it's natural. We have to be naked to shift or we'd never have any clothes. I have shifted fully clothed when I was younger. It wasn't pretty. It happened at a party—another kid was teasing my sister and then he pushed her. She ended up falling and scraping her knees, and seeing the blood set my tiger off. Now of course she can defend herself, but I'm her brother, and no one touches my siblings. I not only scared the kid, but I scared myself. Thank God we were out playing in the forest and there were no humans around.

After our parents leave, we all start getting ready to go outside. Calliope checks to make sure there's no humans around.

"Looks good outside and I don't smell any humans. I do smell some animals. Foxes, coyotes, bobcats and...our parents." She laughs.

Everyone laughs, then we all get undressed. I would be lying if I said seeing my mate naked doesn't affect me. And well, it's kinda hard to hide. Dammit. I can hear my siblings snickering at me. And if it was them? I'd be doing the same. Fuck me.

"You guys go. I need a minute." I sigh.

"Sure." Georgios snickers.

Seriously? I roll my eyes at them as they leave. Then I realize Artemis has stayed back with me. Fuck, she's gorgeous. I walk over to her and kiss her. It's not like she doesn't know what she's doing to me.

Artemis reaches down and wraps her hands around my cock.

"Baby," I whisper.

She drops to her knees and licks the tip of my cock. I swear I'm going to come just from that.

Artemis

Seeing Kostas' hard cock has me dripping wet. I can't help it. I drop to my knees and lick the tip. He moans, and it's my new favorite sound. I take him into my mouth as far as I can and slide my hands around the rest. I've never given anyone a blow job before, and I'm hoping I'm doing it right. By the sounds he's making, I think I'm doing just fine.

We've talked about how we're both virgins. So this is new for both of us, and it makes me happy. I never thought he'd be a virgin. I'm glad he is, and this is something we'll get to experience together. I want him to take me and fuck me now, but I don't think it's a good idea with everyone nearby.

When I saw him naked, I had to touch him.

"Fuck yes, baby," he moans as he's sliding himself in and out of my mouth slowly.

I can feel myself dripping, and I hear him growl as he takes a deep breath.

"I can smell you," he says through gritted teeth. He pulls me up and kisses me roughly.

I reach between us and stroke him. At the same time, he reaches down between us and runs his fingers over my clit. Fuck, having him touch me where only I've touched me...

"Oh god, baby," I gasp. "I'm going to come."

"Me too, fuck yes," he growls as he shoots onto my stomach. Right as I feel it, I come with him.

We're both breathing hard, and he wraps his arms around me as we slow it down.

"Holy shit, that was amazing," he says.

I nod. "I might spontaneously combust when we finally have sex."

He chuckles and kisses my head.

"When I finally make love to you, it's going to make the gods weep," he whispers.

We head into the bathroom and clean up.

"Do you think they're waiting outside?" I ask.

"Nah, I bet everyone has shifted and left. We'll find them. Let me take a peek outside and make sure there's no humans," he says as he walks to the door. "Looks good. I only smell other animals. Are you ready to meet my tiger?"

"I've been waiting for both of you my whole life." I smile as I reach up and kiss him.

When I was little, I dreamt of finding my fated mate. My parents and grandparents found theirs. My brothers and I used to talk about it. None of them have found theirs. They've also never had serious relationships, but when they do find their mate? Fated or chosen, I know they're going to be the best husbands.

As we step outside, I take a deep breath in. I love being in the forest. It reminds me of home, and I miss home a lot. We move towards the forest line and start to stretch out. I watch Kostas, he's so damn sexy. I've learned that it's easier for me to shift if I sit and breathe slowly. I feel my bear start to take over and my bones shift. It's not a bad pain, but it's definitely uncomfortable. My shift takes about two minutes, and now my bear is out and happy. I sit and wait for Kostas to come over. His tiger is purring at me, and my bear is purring right back. I'm twice his size in my bear form, so I wrap my arms around him. The connection I feel with him is incredible. I stretch again, and we make our way deeper into the forest.

In human form, I'm able to smell and sense things that regular humans can't. In my bear form, it's like a whole new world. Colors are brighter, smells are stronger, and I feel more alive. If I could live in my bear form, I probably would.

Going deeper into the forest, out of the corner of my eye, I see a white fluff barreling towards me. Now, I'm pretty fast, but because I'm focusing on Kostas, I get blindsided by Eros. He slams into me, and we roll for a few feet. That evil shit. He's laughing, which sounds like wheezing. Maybe he'll pass out because it doesn't even sound like he's getting enough oxygen. Now he's rolling around still making that noise. I huff and walk back towards Kostas, trying to shake off the dirt and leaves stuck to me. That's when I notice that Kostas is laughing too. I glare at him, which only makes him and my brothers laugh more.

Calliope comes up next to me and nudges me to follow her. She leads me to a clearing with a huge pond. We jump in and swim around. Calliope is a gorgeous white tiger with black stripes. Her stripes are thinner than Kostas', and Georgios' stripes are the thickest. They're beautiful and so unique. I can't wait to see what their parents look like. As polar bears, people think we have white fur, but we don't. Our fur is transparent and so we can be different colors. It's kind of like a camouflage where we blend into our surroundings. So right now? I'm a greenish color because of the forest and the water.

The area that we're in is secluded, which nice. I don't hear or smell any humans. And after a while, our parents join us. Seeing Kostas' parents, they're just as gorgeous as their kids, which makes sense because they made them. Panagiotis has thick, bold stripes that make him look almost completely black. And Stella? She's almost pure white—her stripes are so thin and delicate, they're barely visible.

Seeing our families together makes me wonder what our kids will look like. Will they be polar bears? Or tigers? In rare instances, a child can be born with both animals. That would be a dream come true, to have our children be dual animals.

Kostas comes up and nuzzles me. He's still laughing at me along with my brothers. I do my best to squint at him. He gives me the saddest look a tiger could make. I can't keep the scowl on my face, and I purr at him. Dammit. He purrs back, and we all get out of the pond to do more exploring. We spend time chasing each other around and unfortunately run into some humans. Kostas' parents were chasing each other and stumbled onto a hiking trail. Before we could smell them, there was a family of humans. His parents froze and stared at them. We all watch the humans slowly back away—they're surprisingly calm. When they're gone, we take one more dip in another lake, and this one has a small waterfall. It looks like most of the ponds here are connected by the river. That's the way it is on the Cimaruta MC property too. There's seven beautiful ponds, and they're all connected by a crystal-clear river. We've walked around the property a lot since we've been here. It's so peaceful. Just like here on the Mancini property.

We all make our way back to the cabin and shift back one at a time to avoid getting caught. Kostas and I wait to shift and spend some time cuddling together. I love his tiger. He's trying to wrap himself around me, but he can't. Eventually, I sit on him. He rumbles under me and finally tosses me off him. I huff, and he smiles at me. Or what I perceive as smiling for a tiger. His tongue is hanging out of his mouth. I'm trying to be annoyed that he threw me off of him, but I just can't. He's too damn adorable.

After we've all shifted back and are sitting in the cabin, I finally get to really look at everyone.

My family and my new family. As of now we are our own clan, earlier in the day, our fathers were discussing the idea that we would stay in Chicago as a family. All because of Artemis and me. "We should head back to the main house," Panagiotis says to everyone.

Chapter Eight

Kostas

It was hard to say goodbye to Artemis last night. It feels like I've known her my whole life, but in reality, it's only been two days. This mating bond is no joke. I never thought it would be like this. I don't know anyone who is a fated mate. Artemis has been lucky, she's watched her parents and grandparents with theirs. She said that even watching them didn't prepare her for how strong these feelings are. Even when we're not together, I can feel her. Like a homing beacon that's leading me to her at all times. And when we're together, that bond vibrates between us.

"How are you doing, Son?" my dad asks me.

"I'm okay, Dad. I still can't believe I found Artemis. It's like I'm in a dream, and it's all going to vanish when I wake up."

"Your mamá and I are so happy that you've met your mate. That's always been our dream—for you, Georgios and Calliope to find your mates. I love your mamá, and I could never imagine being with someone else. But we've talked about what would happen if we met ours too."

I never really thought about the fact that my parents aren't fated. They're chosen mates. They've always known that they could meet their fated ones at anytime. Now I wonder what they would do if that happened.

"What would you do? If you were to find your fated one?" I ask him.

"Honestly? I don't know what I would do. I love your mamá so much, and I would lay down my life for her. But I've heard that the fated bond is so strong...well, I just don't know. She's my heart."

I nod at my dad. When I was chosen to be with Xenia, I dreaded having to spend the rest of my life with her. There was a small part of me that had hoped one day, maybe I could love her. Looking back now, we would've been miserable. Forever.

"I can feel Artemis even now. It's like a

constant connection. I can't hear her, but I can feel her. It's so hard to put into words how it feels. I do know that even if I was still with Xenia, I would've left her when I found Artemis. I have no doubt about that."

My dad smiles at me. "Since you and Artemis have found each other, Zeus and I were talking, and we agreed that finding a property that we can all share is the best way to go forward. We're connected now, and this way we can all get to know each other better. We're planning on looking at a couple today. Each of them have two main houses and room to build more. The first will be a house for you and Artemis."

"Thank you, Dad. We really appreciate that. It's been so hard to say goodbye to her these last two days." I laugh. "Has It really only been two days? It feels like a lifetime already."

Dad laughs with me. "Once we find our new home, we will plan your wedding and have a big celebration."

"I can't wait. I didn't think I was ready to be someone's husband, but after finding Artemis? I can't wait to be a husband and a dad."

My dad smiles at me. "You're going to make a great husband and dad. I'm so proud of the man you've become."

I hug him. He's my role model, and if I can be even half the man he is? I'll be okay. Dad has taught us that everything we do has consequences. Sure, we make mistakes, but we learn from them. I hope I don't make too many with Artemis. Even though we're mates, it doesn't mean we can't fuck it all up. I've heard losing your mate for any reason is the worst pain you can go through. I don't ever want to feel that.

Artemis

I hate saying goodbye to Kostas. Watching him walk away hurts my soul. Earlier, my dad told us that we would all be finding a place to live together. Our clan and Kostas' will be one. I'm so excited.

We're on our way out of the arena, and we'll be headed back to the Cimaruta MC property. When someone grabs me from behind, I turn and pull my arm back to hit whoever is touching me.

"Baby, please," I hear Aion plead.

I yank my arm out of his grasp.

"I'm not your baby, don't fucking touch me."

"We're meant to be together. You know it and I know it. Fuck, our families planned our wedding!"

I snort. "We aren't meant to be anything. You were never my mate; you were the one I chose. And now I know I chose wrong. Kostas is my mate, and if you can't accept that? Then I don't know what to tell you, except that you need to move on because even if he wasn't my mate? I would *never* take you back. You made your choice with Daphne, and I made mine. Never again."

"You'll figure out that Kostas isn't what you think he is," he snarls at me.

"What the fuck is that supposed to mean?"

"Tigers shouldn't mix with bears, and you know it. So mate or not? You two are never going to work out." The way he spits out 'mate' makes me want to rip his throat out.

"My tiger mate is more of a man than you'll ever be. Fuck off and deal with your own shit."

I turn to walk away, and again, he grabs my arm. I swing around and kick him in the solar plexus.

"I warned you," I say as I walk away. My brothers were running over just as I kicked Aion. They pull up short and start smiling. I love my brothers, but I can take care of myself when I need to and they know it. It's nice to know they always have my back, though. Just like I'll always have theirs.

"What did that shithead want?" Ares asks.

"Same old shit, telling me we're supposed to be together and that Kostas and I are wrong for thinking we're fated mates."

My brothers laugh.

"I always knew there was something wrong with him. And now I know for sure because he's stupid enough to ignore the fact that you found your fated mate. Not just your chosen one."

"I just want him to leave me alone. He implied that Kostas is a bad person, but I know that's his jealousy talking. Aion thinks he's better than Kostas because he's a bear. Well, fuck him and his cheating bear. I told Aion I wouldn't take him back even if I hadn't found Kostas."

They all hug me.

"Good. Because he never deserved you anyway. He's always acted like he was better than you and us too. I'm glad he's out of the picture," Eros declares.

"Did you hear? We're going to be buying property with the Nikolaidis family," Ares says.

"We are? Like one big property and we all live in the same house?" I ask.

"No. One property, two main houses, and we plan to build you and Kostas your own home," our dad says, coming up to us.

I'm pretty sure I heard my dad wrong.

"Won't that be too much money? We can wait to build a house." I cock my head and look up at my dad.

"No, kardia mou, I meant what I said. Zeus and I will be building a house for you and Kostas to call your own. And the property will have enough room for everyone to eventually have their own house as you find your mates. Fated or chosen."

I wrap my arms around my dad.

"Thank you so much. That's more than I could ever dream of."

"You're welcome, kardia mou. I'm so happy you and Kostas have found each other."

"Me too, Baba. After I caught Aion and Daphne, I told myself I didn't need anyone. But Kostas? I need him. Like the air I breathe."

My dad hugs me tighter and kisses my head.

"We're headed out in about thirty minutes to look at a few properties, did you all want to go?" he asks us.

We all say yes, then scatter to grab our stuff. I love the Bastianini property. I hope the one we find is close by and similar to theirs. I've gotten to know Isabella and Luciana better, and I can't wait to spend more time with them. They've introduced me to their friends and they've embraced me like

I've always been part of their group. They've even started to include Calliope in our get togethers. Their friends don't know that we're shifters, but maybe one day we'll tell them.

"I like the second property. That one had a few small ponds and one big one. And as an added bonus? We're right between the Mancini and Bastianini properties. It looked like we could ask them permission to open up the middle part and make one big forest," Zeus says.

"Maybe we should ask Giacomo and Enea to look at it. It wouldn't hurt to get their opinions."

Everyone agrees, and my dad gets on the phone to call Giacomo while Zeus calls Enea.

Within two hours, we've made our decision. The property we picked backs up against both of their properties. Enea and Giacomo have expanded their properties to match ours. We will share the forest area, and there will still be camping and recreation that the Mancini's have been offering. There's just more land for it now.

Everyone's excited because this means that no matter the outcomes of our trial fights, we will all be staying in Chicago. And we now have a safe space to shift and run. Sure, we need to make sure we watch for humans, but that's okay. We're used to that already.

The realtor said that it usually takes a month to be able to move in. But since no one is living on the property and hasn't for a while, we can move in now. This property is perfect. Even the main houses fit our families. The larger house will be for us because we have more people in our family and the other for the Nikolaidis family.

Chapter Nine

Kostas

It's been a month since we moved to Chicago and I met my mate. Artemis. She's strong and feisty, yet soft and loving. She's everything I could've ever hoped for in a mate. As a newly-formed clan, we have found the perfect property and have been living on it for almost two weeks. It feels like we have the best of both worlds now. We will start building the home that Artemis and I will share in a few weeks. Until it's done, we're still living with our families. We've also agreed to wait to have our wedding till after it's built. That also means we'll wait to have sex. I want the first time we're together to be in the home we'll share for the rest of our lives. I didn't realize how hard it would be. Every moment I'm with her is torture. My tiger doesn't really understand why we're waiting, and he gets really grumpy about it. Okay, both of us are grumpy about it, but at least I understand why.

My siblings and I have been formally invited to fight in the SMMA, and so has Artemis and all of her brothers. Unfortunately, so have Aion and his siblings, *and* as if things weren't uncomfortable enough with him being around, Xenia is here. She and her siblings were given an invitation after we left Greece. Apparently the SMMA wants more female fighters. I get that, but why her? I had hoped to never see her again.

Today we all have to go to the orientation at the Combine Center, where the Chicago Redhawks play. They're the home hockey team. Their season starts next month, and I can't wait to go to the games. Three of their star players are part of the Mancini family.

After getting to the arena, of course the first people we see are Xenia and her family. For fuck's sake.

"Congratulations to your cubs on qualifying for the SMMA," Lazaros Makros says to my dad.

My dad nods at him. "Thank you, and congratulations to you and your family too."

I kiss Artemis' head. I know she's keeping tabs on Xenia, just like I'm doing with Aion.

"Hi, love," we hear Xenia say from behind us.

I don't know why our exes insist on hanging on when they know damn fucking well that what they did to us was the end of it. I ignore Xenia and focus on frowning at Aion instead.

"Why are you ignoring me? I tried to call you yesterday. We really need to talk," she continues on.

Okay, fine. I guess I need to tell her again why I don't have time for her.

"We have nothing to talk about, Xenia."

"Oh, we have lots to talk about, Kostas. So maybe you should tell your little friend here that she needs to take a walk."

Just as I'm about to answer her, Artemis speaks up.

"Anything you have to say to Kostas, you can

say in front of me. There's nothing you can do or say to make me walk away from him."

Artemis isn't a small woman; she stands five foot ten and probably has twenty-five pounds more muscle on her versus Xenia's five-foot-five frame.

"My mate and I need to talk, and I won't talk in front of a bitch like you," Xenia snaps at Artemis.

Artemis bursts out laughing. "Your 'mate'? Now that's the funniest thing I've heard all morning."

"Fuck you, bear-freak. You need to walk away."

And I'm done with this whole conversation.

"No, Xenia, you're the one who needs to walk away. I'm going to say this once. Artemis is my fated mate. My only mate. So if you can't speak to her with respect? Don't speak to either of us at all."

The look on Xenia's face is priceless. She's not used to not getting her way. And from what I've seen of her? She thinks all men want her.

"You're lying. She's a fucking bear. There's no way the fates would pair a tiger with a piece-of-shit bear."

I can feel Artemis vibrating, and that means her bear is trying to take over. I need to get her out of here before she does. I push past Xenia and take Artemis outside.

"Look at me, Marshmallow," I say softly.

She frowns at me. "Did you just call me a fucking 'marshmallow'?"

She's starting to breathe slower, and I smile at her.

"Yes, I did."

She growls. "I'm no marshmallow, you weirdo."

I laugh and kiss her. "When I first saw you shift, all I could see was a beautiful fluffy white bear. My tiger thought you looked like a tasty marshmallow when you ran, and he loved chasing you."

She giggles. I love the blush that's spreading across her cheeks. "Did he really think that?"

I hug her tight. "He did, and he kept saying that you're probably just as delicious as a marshmallow."

"Your tiger is lucky he's so damn sexy." She holds me tight. "So, that bitch is your ex, huh?"

I sigh. "Yes. That's Xenia, I don't know why she'd want to talk to me now. She was never interested even when we were paired together."

"She probably realizes what she's lost and wants you back."

"Well, tough shit for her. Even if I didn't have you, I wouldn't take her back."

"I don't know if you noticed, but she had a funny scent to her."

I nod. "I did notice that, but I don't know what it was. Knowing her, she's planning something. She doesn't know how to take 'no' for an answer."

"Should I be worried?" Artemis asks, looking up at me.

"No, Marshmallow. I'm yours and only yours. Just like you're mine. There's no one that could ever make me leave you."

I lean down and touch my lips to hers. I run my tongue along her lips, asking for her to let me in. When she does, it makes me moan. I hear her purring as we deepen the kiss.

"Why did we agree to wait again?" I chuckle as I pepper her face with more kisses.

"Right now I'm not sure. My bear is stomping around saying I was stupid to agree to that."

"My tiger is feeling the same way. Maybe we shouldn't wait," I whisper, nuzzling right below her ear. I've found that this spot makes her growl, and I love it.

"I don't want to either, but I want our first time to be something to remember forever," she says softly while she moans.

Fuck, I need to stop. I already know I love her and want only her, but I also know she's right. I want our first time to be the best experience for both of us. Once we have sex, we will have our mating bite. As shifters, we can do the mating bite with others that aren't our fated mates. But from what I've heard from the stories and from what Artemis has told me about her parents? The mating bite between fated mates is one out of fairytales. I can't fucking wait.

Artemis

I can't believe I let that tramp get to me. How could I have done that? Fuck! I know in every fiber of my being that Kostas would never hurt me, or leave me. But after the whole thing with Aion and Daphne, I feel more vulnerable. I'm second-guessing my real mate and I hate it.

I look into Kostas' deep-green eyes—the color reminds me of Christmas. It's like they're changing colors as I look at them. He makes me feel calm, and I can't stand that I let that bitch make me second guess him and his love for me. She'll never get the best of me again.

"It's you and me against the exes." I sigh.

Kostas nods. "It's you and me against everything, Marshmallow."

I haven't decided if I like this 'marshmallow'

thing. I do know I like his explanation on how it became his term of endearment for me. So maybe I'll let it slide and be his marshmallow. Even though I don't like to eat them.

"Do you know if Xenia is going to be fighting?" I ask him.

"I have no idea. I didn't even know they got an invitation. She's never even hinted that she or her sisters liked to fight. I knew Viktor, her brother, was a fighter."

I sigh again. "I wish they weren't here. I know that's selfish because this is an opportunity for all shifters. But I wish Aion's and Xenia's families were later, not at the same time as us."

"I feel the same way, baby. We just need to do our best to ignore them."

"I'll try. I'm sorry I let her get to me, I'm not usually like that." I frown.

"Don't worry, Artemis. Xenia can bring those feelings out in anyone. Including my sister. It's not just you, Calliope was angry all the time when she lived with us."

I chuckle. "I can't even imagine living with her. In just those few minutes, I wanted to claw her eyes out. And when she was insulting me, my bear was roaring."

"I felt you start to vibrate, that's why I knew I

needed to get you outside. But we need to go back in. Are you ready to face them again?"

I reach up and kiss him, I love his lips. "Yes. Thank you for taking care of me."

"I'll be taking care of you for the rest of our lives. Which if we're lucky, will be hundreds of years."

"It will be. You're not allowed to ever leave me."

"Never. I would never dream of leaving you."

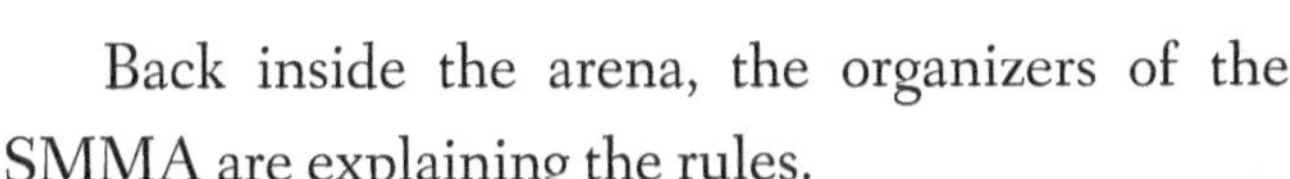

Back inside the arena, the organizers of the SMMA are explaining the rules.

"There will be no shifting during the fight. That rule is one that if broken, you will be disqualified and banned from ever fighting in the SMMA again. We have no way to keep humans out of the crowds for the fights. If you feel like you need to shift before or after your fight, let us know. We have a designated area downstairs made specifically for that."

The unbreakable rule is one we all knew before

coming for the tryouts. Here in America, we've been told that some humans have heard rumors about shifters. And there are some that know, but not enough for us to come out into the open and reveal who we truly are. This is also why those animal attacks that Salvatore told us about when we first got here are so dangerous. Not just for the humans getting hurt, but for us as shifters.

"Another rule that should go without saying—our secret as shifters is an important one. We can't predict who will be okay with it and who won't. Be smart about who you talk to and where you're having conversations with each other."

"Will we be getting our fighting schedules soon?" another shifter asks.

Being shifters, we're scheduled more frequently than humans. Humans fight two to four times a year. We fight once a month, sometimes more. This is because we heal fast from most things, where humans need more time to train and heal. There are only a few things that would take us longer to heal from. One is massive blood loss. Depending on how fast our blood is lost, we can heal from it. Although it does take a lot longer the faster we lose it. But just fighting? That's an easy fix, one day and we're back to training.

"You'll get your schedules this week. Everyone

here is classified in the 'amateur' category to start. We might move some of you to 'professional' after we see how your initial fights go. Everyone is allowed to use the gym twenty-four hours a day, seven days a week. You just need your credentials to get into the arena, which you'll get today before you leave. But if we find that you're actually fighting each other and not just sparring and working out, first time you will get a cut in pay. Second time, you will get suspended from certain fights. And if there's a third time, you will be out of the SMMA. We don't bend the rules for anyone."

Kostas

I can feel eyes on me, and I look over to see Aion looking at us from one side and then Xenia looking from the other. In a perfect world, they would both still be back in Greece. But this is what Artemis and I will have to deal with. She's told me what Aion did, and I told her what Xenia did. It was worse for Artemis because not only did Aion betray her, her best friend did too. For me, I never wanted to be with Xenia. So finding her with Casper didn't affect me the same way. Artemis had her heart broken by two people who should've cared for her. And from what she knows, Daphne is now pregnant with Aion's cub. Which of course he denies.

"Okay, I think that's it. You will all receive an email with your schedules. The first fights won't start for two weeks. That will give you time to get settled and start training. Good luck to all of you! And don't forget to pick up your ID card before you leave."

Artemis and I head over to the table to pick up our credentials. Just as we get there, Aion pushes into me. I know he's doing it to make me fight him. I can't let him get to me, even though my tiger is roaring so loud it's hurting my head. I tell him that there will be plenty of opportunities for us to fight in the ring. It's just a matter of time.

As we walk away from the table, Xenia blocks our path. We try to step around her.

"You can't keep ignoring me, Kostas," her voice is rising as she speaks.

"I'm not ignoring you, Xenia. We have just nothing to talk about. Everything that needed to be said was said back in Greece."

"That's not true. Something happened after you left Greece." She glares at Artemis.

I sigh. "Anything that happened after I left

Greece is between you and whoever you're with now. Not me."

She cackles at me. "You're going to be a daddy, Kostas."

I frown and feel Artemis tense up next to me. I grip her hand tighter.

"There is no fucking way that you're pregnant by me. Zero. None. So don't even start this bullshit."

"You know this cub is yours, Kostas. You're just saying that because this bitch won't let go of you."

"No, I'm saying this because it's the truth. And I won't have you lying about me or my family."

Xenia starts laughing. Hysterically. It's embarrassing because everyone is starting to stare at us. We need to get the fuck away from her.

I pull Artemis away, and we head towards our families.

"KOSTAS NIKOLAIDIS! You can't ignore me and our cub!"

Holy crap. My family and Artemis' are now staring at us and Xenia. Xenia's family steps up to her and takes her outside.

"If she's pregnant? It's not mine," I reassure Artemis. "I never touched her. Not even to hold her hand."

Artemis nods at me. "I believe you."

Relief floods me as I look into her eyes. She truly believes me—there's no doubt there. I lean down and kiss her.

"You and me against the exes," she whispers.

I smile as I hold her. "You and me against the exes."

"What is wrong with that psycho?" Calliope says as she comes up to us.

"She's a fucking nightmare." Artemis sighs.

"You should've seen how it was when she came to stay with us. You think this was bad?" Calliope laughs.

Chapter Ten

Artemis

Xenia wasn't lying about being pregnant, and she's made it her mission to tell everyone she can that Kostas left her knowing she was pregnant. She comes to his fights and cheers for him like they're still together. I've been fighting once a week, and I've won every time. I think the anger I feel towards Xenia helps. Because I have a lot.

Not that Aion's been any better. He's been trying to push Kostas' buttons. They haven't fought each other yet, but it's coming.

The animal attacks are getting more frequent. When we got here, there had been five in the last two years. These last few months, there's been one every month. The humans think a tiger's responsible because of the teeth and claw marks. That scares me even more because Kostas' family are tigers. What if someone sees him or one of his family? And then there's the hunters, saying they should be allowed to hunt the killer. I don't like where any of this is going.

Today Salvatore is coming over to our place to give us an update and show us whatever evidence he can. Maybe we'll get lucky and at least be able to scent what type of animal or shifter it is.

An hour later, our house is filled with the four families. It's loud, and I love it.

"So these are the only things I could bring with me," Salvatore says. "Everything has been tested already, but I still can't take it out of the bags. In case we need it for court."

There are photos of the different crime scenes and pieces of clothing in bags. Each of us pick up the bags one by one and sniff them. It takes a little while, then we all sit down to discuss our thoughts.

"It's definitely a shifter," my dad says.

We all nod and agree.

"Are you able to tell what kind of shifter?" Salvatore asks.

"I hate to say this, but it smells like a tiger." Panagiotis sighs.

Everyone quietly agrees, and it makes me scared for the Nikolaidis family. For my Kostas. We need to come up with a plan to track the killer. And make sure he or she can't hurt anyone ever again.

"Are you sure it's a shifter and not just a rogue tiger?" asks Mac Walker, Salvatore's partner.

Last week we had to let Salvatore tell Mac about us being shifters. This situation is already an ongoing investigation and not just a rumor of attacks. He took the news better than most humans do, and just like when we told the Mancinis and Bastianinis, we had to shift for it to really sink in.

I think Mac was a little scared. I mean, having seven polar bears and five tigers in front of you at the same time can be a little intimidating. But he handled it really well. He said that our eyes stay the same, so he could tell we were still in there.

"If we can go to the most recent attack site, we can try to get a scent," my dad suggests.

"It's still being investigated. But as soon as they're done, we can take you there," Mac says.

"The problem with that is the scent could fade by then. Just like when you collect evidence, the sooner the better," Panagiotis explains.

"I understand that. Maybe we can work something out. The last attack happened a week ago. Do you think you can still get a scent off that?" Salvatore asks.

Dad thinks for a minute, "We can try. A week is pushing it, but our abilities are above average, so it's possible."

"I'll make a call and see who's on the scene tonight. There might be less security because of the time of day," Mac says as he's walking away to make his phone calls.

"Since we can't all go to the scene, we need to pick our best trackers," Stella says. "Calliope is the best at tracking scents in our family."

"Apollo is best in ours," my mamá says.

"Okay, so once Mac gets the info, Calliope and Apollo will go with us to the scene," Salvatore says.

"We need to shift to have the best chance at sniffing out the killer," Apollo says.

Salvatore nods. "We'll find you a place."

"Okay, looks like they're pulling the guards at

about ten tonight. We can head over and see what we can find," Mac says.

We all agree and set out to have a barbecue in the meantime.

Kostas

Knowing that the attacks are being done by a tiger shifter makes me angry. We already have so many things we have to be careful about and these attacks are making things worse. Now that we know it's a tiger shifter, the next step is tracking him or her without exposing ourselves.

The people that come to our campgrounds are more cautious now. They say they're afraid of coming across the animals that roam our lands. We do our best to reassure them that as long as they stay on the trails, they should be okay. Because there are wild animals out here, they do have to be careful. Now if they came up against a shifter, that's a different situation. We know who we are even in our animal form, and that means we can avoid humans. Or it at least we won't attack them.

We do have rules for the people that come to stay on the properties. There's no shooting of any kind, they can carry bear spray and even a taser, but no guns or bows. We even provide air horns so they can scare away an animal if they see it. We don't want them killing any animals that are roaming around. So far, the people that come and stay abide by the rules. Enea Mancini says that he's had a few issues with customers, but for the most part? They respect the rules.

It's hard to relax and eat when I know what's at stake. If we don't help find this killer—I hope it's just one—then this is going to keep going on. And one day it could seriously impact us as a clan. When I was younger, I wished that humans could know about us. But now that I'm an adult, I see why we keep it a secret. Humans aren't equipped to deal with shifters. Their first instinct is to kill. Or experiment on us. And now with these murders? It's an even worse situation. People are panicking and looking for solutions, and I'm afraid their solution will be to kill first and ask questions later.

Waiting for them to come back from the scene is excruciating. I know the killer's not one of our clan. We've met the other shifters in the SMMA, and I'm hoping that it's not one of them. I want it to be a rogue shifter, because if it's one of the fighters? Then they're just murdering humans for sport. Which isn't unheard of, it's just fucked up. At least rogue shifters can't really help it.

It feels like we've been waiting for days, but when I look at the clock, it's only been two hours. I'm not made to be patient. My tiger is restless, and I can feel the tension from everyone here. Maybe we should go for a run? But then again, we can't. What if they come back while we're out? Fuck.

We wait another two hours before Calliope texts to say they're on their way back. And we're not going to like what they found. Again, fuck.

They're finally back, and we've all been going crazy from waiting.

"Spill it!" Georgios yells as they walk in the door. He scares all four of them, and the three men shove Calliope behind them, protecting her...I think. I bust out laughing. My sister can take anyone down, and they're protecting her.

"What the fuck, Georgios!" Calliope growls at him, then goes over and punches him in the arm. "Dumbass."

"Watch that language," our mamá says to her.

"Yes, mamá. Sorry," Calliope says. Then she glares at Georgios as he snickers as quietly as he can.

The rest of us are almost on the floor laughing, even the parents.

"Let's go and sit in the living room. Then you can tell us what you found," Zeus says.

It takes a minute for everyone to get situated. I wrap my arms around Artemis as she leans back into me. I can feel how nervous she is. I feel the same.

"Okay, so when we first got to the scene, before we shifted, I could already smell that a shifter had been there," Apollo starts.

"And I could smell that that shifter was a tiger. So now we know for sure," Calliope adds. "We decided to shift anyway and see if we could get a trail or see if the scent was familiar in any way."

I hate that my sister is drawing this out. Because she's doing it on purpose, judging by the look on her face.

"Okay, just say it." Our Dad sighs.

Calliope smiles. "There were two scents. Not just one. But I feel like the problem is, we don't know if it's been the same shifters the whole time. I mean, the first killings were two years ago, and those were farther apart. Now it's every other week. Why? And it only started to escalate when all of us moved here. And I don't mean *us*, I mean the new group that's fighting with the SMMA."

"You might be onto something, it was right after everyone came for the tryouts that it got worse," Mac replies.

"So what does that mean for us?" Eros asks.

"It means we need to be extra vigilant when we're shifting." My mamá answers.

"Do you think you would know their scent if you ran into them?" Salvatore asks.

"Maybe. Sometimes when you've been with your clan as long as we have, everyone ends up smelling like each other."

"So it's not like a fingerprint where each shifter has their own scent?" Mac asks.

"No. I wish it was that simple. But it's not," my dad says.

"What we do know after tonight is that the earlier attacks might not be connected to the recent ones." Salvatore sighs. "I'll have to get the files for all the attacks and look them over. We should be able to figure it out."

"Please keep us updated. And if we can help more, we will," my dad responds.

Chapter Eleven

Artemis

Kostas is still calling me 'Marshmallow', and my family thinks it cute. My bear? She's on the fence about it. He called her that once when I had shifted before him. She spent the entire run glaring at him, but that hasn't stopped him.

There's been more attacks, and they're getting more frequent. They went from once every few months, to once a month, and now it's twice a month. We should be able to catch the killer, but it hasn't been easy. Somehow, this shifter has been able to block their scent. It's so damn frustrating. We should be able to find them.

Kostas and his family come over to our house every morning for breakfast.

"Salvatore is headed over with Mac. He says there's something he needs to talk to us about," my dad says to everyone.

"Has there been a break in the case?" Athena asks.

"I'm not sure, he wouldn't tell me over the phone. He sounds worried."

We finish eating while we wait for Salvatore. It's always the waiting that's the worst, especially when you don't know what to expect.

Finally, there's an alert from the front gate. We watch Salvatore drive up to our house.

Eros opens the door before he can knock and invites him in. After we all get our hugs in, we stare at him, waiting.

Salvatore sighs. "Someone came in and made an accusation about who could be doing the killings. He didn't say anything about shifters, but he did say that it's a tiger."

I'm trying to keep my voice steady. "Who came in and who did they point the finger at?"

Salvatore looks at me. "His name is Aion Calimeris, and he pointed the finger at Kostas. He told the detective who took his statement that he's seen you with a few white tigers."

"Oh for fuck's sake," Apollo mutters. "Aion is an asshole."

"When did this happen?" I ask Salvatore.

"He came in a few days ago with a girl. I tried to catch them after I found out, but they left before I could. I'm guessing you know him?"

"I do. He's my ex and he's an asshole. I can guarantee he did this just to hurt Kostas."

Salvatore nods at me. "I'll let the other detectives know that. That's an important fact—that he's an angry ex. It makes his statement less viable."

I let out a sigh of relief, but my relief is short-lived.

"I'm still going to have to bring Kostas in for questioning. And I won't be able to be the one to question him."

Well fuckity-fuck.

"It's okay, I have nothing to hide," Kostas says. "When do you need me to come in?"

"How does tomorrow morning sound? And I have to warn you, the lead detective on this is a hard-ass. He's not a bad cop, he just thinks he knows best. So he's probably going to come down on you."

Kostas nods at Salvatore. "Thanks for the

heads-up. Like I said, I'm innocent, so he can ask anything."

"Don't offer information. And it might be wise to have a lawyer with you."

"I'll go," Lorenzo Mancini says. He's the youngest Mancini brother and the lawyer for the family.

"Thank you, Lorenzo," Kostas says.

"We take care of each other. I'll pick you up in the morning at ten, and I need you to follow my lead. Don't say anything unless I nod at you to answer."

"Okay, no problem."

I can feel the tension rolling off of Kostas, and the best way I know to help is for us to shift and run.

"If it's okay, I think Kostas and I need to shift," I say to everyone.

"Just be careful, especially with the attacks, you need to be extra vigilant with humans around," my dad warns.

I go over and hug him. "We will, Baba."

Kostas and I head out to the area that we've blocked off on our property for shifting. Right now it's just a tent, but eventually we'll have a structure built. The tent actually makes it easier to detect humans. I don't smell any this time. I watch Kostas get undressed, he's so fucking sexy. I follow him and get my clothes off, folding them and setting them to the side. When I turn back to him, he's stroking his cock.

"You like what you see?" he teases me.

Fuck. Our house is almost done and we've done a decent job waiting to have sex. But times like this is when I question the wait. I walk over to him and wrap my hands around his cock. His growl makes me instantly wet.

"Are we sure we want to wait?" I moan and nip his chest. I can feel the rumble he's making.

Kostas grabs the blanket that's behind me, and lays it on the ground. We lie down together.

"I will wait if you want, and if you don't, I will

make love to you right now," he whispers as he rubs himself on me.

"Kostas..." I moan.

Do I want to feel him in me? Fuck yes. But I want my first time to be in our bed. So I muster all my willpower, which isn't much and look into his eyes.

"You know there's no doubt how much I want you. But I don't want our first time to be here."

He captures my mouth with his and shows me just how much he wants me too.

"We should shift and get out there. I want to run with your tiger." I smile at him.

"Anything you want, Marshmallow."

I laugh and push him off of me. He's such a dork.

I relax and let the shift take me. I can feel my bear stretching and her excitement about being out. Kostas and I sniff around before we poke our heads out of the tent. Still only faint human scents but no animals. Not smelling any big animals is a little weird, we usually get at least a whiff of them. Maybe they're sleeping.

We head out and slowly enter the forest, heading up to the mountain. It's become our favorite place to run. And because the mountainside is steeper than the regular hiking trails, humans don't come up here as much. When we reach the top of the waterfall, there's a gorgeous pond. I run and jump into the water. I swim around as Kostas watches me. I can hear him purring. I swim over to where he's lying at the edge of the pond and jump out. I circle him slowly as my bear senses take over. We crouch down and shove our nose under him, rolling him into the pond before he knows what we're doing. After he splashes in, we jump back in.

When I let my bear take over, I can still feel everything around me. And the connection we feel for Kostas. It's not just the animal connection we have, it's the human one too. It's the feeling that we're connected in our hearts. That my body and soul knows him, he can walk up behind me and I don't have the urge to turn and strike. Because I can feel it's him.

After we swim, we sun on the rocks. I know if anyone sees us it would look pretty weird. A tiger and a polar bear sunning together. But hey, it works for us. I don't know how long we've been out here, but I wake up when I hear voices. Shit. We fell asleep and now we have to make sure we're not found. I nudge Kostas and sniff upwards as he yawns then sniffs. His eyes get really big and he chuffs softly.

We quietly head towards the forest and back to our tent. As soon as we get there, I lie down and let the shift take over.

"That was too close." I say.

He hasn't changed back yet and he's just staring at me. He's so damn beautiful and he's purring at me. And now he's stalking me...my instinct is to shift back to my bear but my body is tired. Kostas backs me into a corner and I swear he's laughing. My bear starts growling at him and he chuffs at me. I do the only thing I can think of. I scratch his head.

At first he's squinting at me, I'm not sure he's ever had his head scratched before. Then all of a sudden he flips on his back and stares at me. What the fuck? Is he asking me to scratch his belly? I frown and go over to him to try it. And he purrs louder than I've heard before. My bear is making noises like she's laughing as I keep scratching his belly. Finally he yawns and stretches, backing away from me. I watch him as he shifts back.

"You're gorgeous." I smile as he pants and lies there catching his breath.

"You're perfect. My tiger wanted to see you and spend time with you," he says as he kisses me.

"My bear wants to do the same, but I didn't know if that would be okay with you."

"Anytime I get to spend with you is great. It doesn't matter if we're in this form or our animals."

I lunge at him and kiss him. I can feel his cock hardening under me as he rubs on me.

"Fuck," I moan.

I'm not sure how much longer I can hold out. I want to feel him in me, and I've never really wanted to have sex with anyone before. It was never a priority. But with Kostas? I want him all day, everyday.

"My tiger is wondering if you taste like a marshmallow," he whispers to me.

It makes me giggle. "I doubt it."

"Soon. I will find out soon," he growls.

Kostas

I've never wanted someone as much as I want Artemis. The hardest part is I know how much she wants me too. Our house is almost done, then we can have our wedding. At first we were going to wait till this rogue shifter was found. After talking with our parents, we decided not to—we'll get married as soon as our house is finished.

I still have to go to the police station, as Lorenzo changed our time to meet with the detective. Salvatore vouched for us, so the detective agreed. I think Salvatore planted some doubt in the other detective's head, which is good because Aion just wants me out of the picture and it's bullshit. The problem is Salvatore hasn't been able to get his hands on Aion's statement. And as confident as I am that Lorenzo and Salvatore can help me, I'm a little scared. What if they pin this on me? What will happen to me? To Artemis? To our families?

I grab Artemis and hold her tight. I kiss her, trying to tell her without words how much she means to me. She rubs herself on me and my tiger goes wild. I'm not sure who wants her more—him or me. Now she's growling and holy fuck...I need to stop this now or my vow to wait will be out the fucking tent.

"Baby, we need to stop or I won't be keeping my promise to you."

She sighs. "I'm so sorry. I don't know how to keep my hands off of you."

"Don't ever apologize for that, Marshmallow. I love that you can't keep you hands off me. Because I can't keep mine off you either."

The smile she gives me makes my heart feel like it's flying. We clean ourselves up and get dressed.

"We should head back to the house. I'm so glad our's is almost done."

We were told that it will be finished next week. Then Artemis will be my wife.

Chapter Twelve

Kostas

I don't know why I'm so nervous as I wait for Lorenzo Mancini to pick me up, I've done nothing wrong. But I've seen stories where someone was falsely accused and went to prison for it. As a shifter, I can't go to prison. There would be no way for me to shift. We can suppress the need, but it could make us go crazy.

I hold Artemis as I work through possible scenarios. Not being able to shift would be nothing compared to not being able to be with her. To hold her, kiss her, feel her arms around me and hear her purr. That would be the thing to would make me go crazy.

I'm so buried in my thoughts about prison and listening to my tiger grumble at me, I don't hear my sister letting Lorenzo in.

"Hey Kostas, are you ready?" Lorenzo asks.

"Oh shit, sorry. I didn't even hear you come in. Yeah, I'm ready. Do you think this detective guy is going to be fair?" I ask.

"I don't know him, but from what Sal said, he's a decent cop. So I think he'll at least listen to what we have to say. He might want to come here and make sure you don't have any animals. Like in cages, not the wild ones."

I nod. "It's okay if he does. We have nothing to hide here."

Turning to Calliope, I say, "Make sure Dad and Mamá know the detective could drop by. I'll try to give you a heads-up if I can."

Calli comes over to me and hugs me tight. "Don't worry about us, we'll be ready."

I know she's worried for me and so is Artemis. I can see it in their eyes.

"We gotta go. Don't worry, it'll be fine," Lorenzo says. He hugs my sister and Artemis, says goodbye to the rest of the family, then heads outside.

I kiss Artemis. "I'll see you when I get back."

She kisses me back. "Be smart. Don't let your anger get the best of you. Remember that's what Aion wants."

"I'll remember, Marshmallow."

She gives me a smile as I leave. Keep calm. Don't let Aion's lies get to me. Got it. I think.

When we get to the station, we have to wait for the detective to show up. Apparently he isn't in yet, even though we had an appointment. Waiting just makes my nerves worse and my tiger is restless because he doesn't understand what's going on.

What feels like hours is probably thirty minutes.

We finally see a man walking towards us. "Detective Carl Reed. You're Kostas Nikolaidis?"

I stand and shake his hand. "I am."

"And you are?" he asks Lorenzo.

"Lorenzo Mancini, I'm Mr. Nikolaidis' attorney."

"Related to Detective Salvatore Mancini?" he asks as he leads us into a room.

"Salvatore's my cousin."

"He's a great detective. You know, Kostas isn't in any trouble, so there's no need for a lawyer."

"It's always safer with a lawyer. And that's no offense to you, Detective."

He stops and looks at the both of us. Then he finally nods.

"That is true. Have a seat. Can I get either of you anything to drink?"

We both decline. I wish I could ask if we can hurry up and get this over with. But that might make me look guilty.

"First off, thank you for coming in. I'm sure you've heard of the animal attacks that have been happening. I had a gentleman come in who named you as a person of interest."

"We would like to know who is accusing Kostas of this." Lorenzo says.

"His name is Aion Calimeris and he wasn't accusing Mr. Nikolaidis. He says he was giving us a heads-up about the fact that he had seen him with tigers. And the attacks *are* being done by an animal, DNA tests have narrowed it down to tigers."

Lorenzo looks at me and nods. We talked about this in the car so I knew what to say.

"I don't know why Aion would say that I've been seen with tigers. My family and I just moved here six months ago. And I don't really know Aion."

"He said he knows you. That you're both from Greece and knew each other there," Detective Reed says.

I shake my head no. "I've talked to Aion once since moving here to Chicago. I never knew him in Greece."

"Then I don't understand why he would single you out. But even so, I still have to check all leads."

"I understand. I should tell you that Aion is my fiancée's ex-boyfriend and he's not happy about the 'ex' part. That's probably his motivation for volunteering that information. And I will help any way I can, but I don't know how. I don't own tigers, and the only ones I've seen here are at the zoo."

Detective Reed nods his head as he writes in his notepad. "Would you consent to me coming to your house so I can see for myself?"

"Yes. But you should know that we own a substantial amount of property with wild animals roaming on it. I can't walking around."

"I understand that. I'm more concerned about animals being kept illegally as pets. Not wild ones, but if we do see wild ones, we need to capture and test them."

"I don't think my dad will agree to that. We have strict rules about the wild animals on our properties."

He frowns slightly at me. "'Properties'? Does your family own more than one?"

I look over at Lorenzo to get the okay to answer that. He nods.

"Our property is connected to the Mancini and Bastianini properties. There is a shared area for campers, hikers and animals to roam."

"That's interesting," he says as he's scribbling on his notepad.

What the fuck is he writing? I can't stand this. He seems nice enough, but the vibe I'm getting from him is that he doesn't believe me. Not that it matters, he'll never find anything to pin the attacks on me or any of our clan.

"When can I come to your property and look around?" he asks.

"You can come today if you want," Lorenzo answers.

Detective Reed nods. "How about I follow you out there now?"

"Sure. Let's go," Lorenzo says.

I know he wants to go now because he thinks

he's going to catch us with something. I'm just glad he'll leave us alone after he sees for himself. And I hope I get paired with Aion for a fight soon. That asshole deserves a beating. Maybe he'll get Georgios or one of Artemis' brothers. Either way, I will enjoy it immensely.

I send a text to Artemis, letting her know that we're headed there with the detective.

Kostas: Marshmallow, we're headed back now. Detective Reed is following us. He wants to take a look around (eyeroll emoji)

Artemis: Okay, my love. I'll let everyone know. How was the interrogation?

Kostas: It was okay. But I think he believes Aion and it's pissing me off

Artemis: (mad face emoji)

> Kostas: We should be there in
> about thirty minutes

> Artemis: Okay. Please drive safe

> Kostas: Always (green heart emoji)

> Artemis: (green heart emoji)

"Should we call Salvatore and let him know what's going on?" I ask Lorenzo as we drive back to the property.

"No, if we do that, it could make it look like you're hiding behind him. And with the feeling I'm getting from Detective Reed? He will definitely take that as you're hiding something. We don't want him coming onto the properties to look whenever he wants."

"True. Fucking Aion. That cowardly piece of shit. I can't fucking believe he would do this. Oh wait, I can."

I'm so angry that Aion did this to me. To all of us. Just so he could get Artemis back, which would never happen even if I wasn't her fated mate. I know she'd never go back to him no matter what. He rejected her and she told me she could never forgive that. And with her best friend. They both betrayed my marshmallow. For me, Xenia's rejection was less hurtful. Not to say it didn't hurt at all, but it wasn't anything like what Artemis went through. I wish I could take that pain from her.

"Did he really do this because he wants Artemis?" Lorenzo asks.

"Yep. That asshole thinks if I'm out of the way, that's his ticket back in. But it doesn't work like that."

"You and Artemis are like soulmates, right?"

"You believe in soulmates?" I ask him.

"I do. I believe there's one person made just for us. And it's a miracle if we find them. I watch my parents everyday and know that's what they are. My twin, Giovanna? She's found her's too, Declan is her perfect other half. And Sebastiano has found his with Schuyler. So you're damn right I believe it."

"That's great. In our culture, we are 'fated mates.' Which is the same as your concept of soulmates. Once we find ours, there is no other. But there are also mates that are chosen. Like my parents. They're chosen mates and have been together for decades."

"What would happen if a chosen mate finds their fated mate?" he asks me.

"That's a hard one. I think it depends on the couple. Like with my parents? I doubt they would ever leave each other. Even if they met their fated one, I think they would deny them and stay together."

"Does that hurt? To reject a fated mate versus a chosen mate?"

"All I know is how I feel. And when I was with Xenia, I wished to find my fated one. She was horrible and I dreaded spending the rest of my life with her. And now that I have Artemis, I would never leave her. But I don't know how it would've been if Aion hadn't rejected her. She would've had to make the choice and there's no guarantee she would've picked me."

I can see him thinking about everything I said.

"That's sad. Especially if you've already chosen a mate, then meet your fated one. That would have to be the hardest decision you'd ever have to make."

"It would be, yes. And I don't wish that on anyone I love."

"Me neither."

We pull into the driveway that leads to our houses. I see all four families standing around in the yard, waiting for us. I guess word spreads fast. Lorenzo is chuckling beside me.

"I guess either Artemis or Calliope put the word out." I laugh.

"That's family for you. We're always there to

back each other up. Plus, my papá and Giacomo Bastianini are very well known in Chicago."

I've heard a few stories about both families. I'm glad they're on our side. Really glad.

We park and get out of the car. Detective Reed parks next to us.

"There's a lot of people here. Are they all family?" Detective Reed asks.

"Yes. We're basically all family here," Enea answers before we can. "I'm Enea Mancini. Mine and Giacomo Bastianini's properties connect directly to this one. So we thought we should all be here if you're going to be inspecting it."

Detective Reed's eyes widen at Enea and Giacomo. He shakes both their hands.

"It's good to meet you both. Salvatore is your son?" he asks Enea.

"No, Lorenzo is my son," he answers. "Salvatore is my nephew. Leonardo is his papá."

"I am Panagiotis Nikolaidis, and Kostas is my son," my dad introduces himself.

"Detective Carl Reed. It's nice to meet you. Kostas gave me permission to take a walk around your property," he says as he shakes my dad's hand.

"What exactly are you looking for?" Dad asks.

"We got a report that you have tigers on your property and I need to see if it's true or not."

"Well, there are wild tigers in the preserve. But none on our personal properties, unless they roam in from the forest."

"Do you keep any in cages?"

"Why would we do that? It's illegal to own them in Illinois, isn't it?"

He nods at my dad. "It is illegal, but that doesn't stop some people from doing it."

"We have no tigers in cages. We will escort you around our personal properties and you will see no cages anywhere. Only fences to keep the campers and hikers out."

Chapter Thirteen

Kostas

It takes a couple of hours for us to show Detective Reed around all private areas of the three properties.

"How many acres do you own total?" he asks my dad.

"Each family owns almost two thousand acres."

"And they're connected in the middle, with entrances and exits between each property?"

"Yes."

Again, Detective Reed is scribbling in his tablet.

"So there could be cages in the forest areas?"

"No. There are no cages anywhere on our property. Only the fences to mark areas that are off limits."

You can hear the anger in my dad's voice. It's like Detective Reed is trying to find a way to pin this on us. I don't understand why. I look at the heads of our families and they all have the same look on their faces.

"You sound like you're trying to imply that our families are keeping illegal animals in cages and hiding them," Lorenzo says as he steps up next to my dad.

Detective Reed frowns. "No, that's not it. I'm saying how can you know about every single thing that happens on the properties? It's a huge area to cover and you may not know what's out there."

"We have a security system and cameras up all over the properties," Sebastiano Mancini, the oldest of Enea's children, speaks up.

"That's illegal. You can't record people on public property," Detective Reed says.

"That would be true if it *were* public property. Our land is private. Not just the areas we live on, but the entire preserve as well. We allow people to come and use our land for recreational purposes. So we are within our rights to have a security system and cameras," Lorenzo says.

There's some snickering coming from our group and I don't think the detective likes that. I'm beginning to like the fact that we have a lawyer in the family.

"I do appreciate you showing me around. I have a few more questions. Do any of you know Aion Calimeris?"

Everyone looks at Lorenzo for the okay to talk. He nods at us.

"He's my ex-boyfriend. We dated when we were still in Greece," Artemis speaks up.

"Is there an ongoing relationship?" Detective Reed looks at Artemis.

"No. There hasn't been for a while now. The relationship ended while we were still in Greece," Artemis answers as she comes to stand next to me.

It looks like the detective might have figured out why Aion would put my name in for these attacks. He nods at us.

"So his report could be because he's jealous?"

"That would be my guess. He learned about Artemis and me a few months ago and of course wasn't happy about it."

"Hmm. Okay. Well again, thank you for your cooperation. I'll be in touch if I need anything else from you."

We watch him get into his car and drive away.

That sucked. I don't think he's going to let this go. I wish Salvatore had been here.

"Let's just hope the killer doesn't strike close to our homes. I don't think that detective is on our side." Zeus sighs.

"I'll call Sal and see what he thinks our next move should be. Because if the timeline holds, there's going to be another killing this week," Lorenzo replies.

"I hope not, but if there is, we need to get Apollo and Calliope to the scene as soon as possible. That's our best chance at getting a scent on them."

Artemis

Could Aion be helping this killer? Just to get Kostas in trouble? I don't want to think he could be capable of doing that. But I can't say for sure that he's not, and it bothers me a lot. Even if you take away the fact that he rejected me. I wouldn't know how to handle it if he turns out to be a killer. Or someone that's willing to set up an innocent person for his own personal gain. This was a man I had fallen in love with, planned a future with. That's a scary thought.

"Are you okay, Artemis?" I hear Kostas ask me, breaking through my introspection.

"I'm okay. It's so weird to think that Aion could have a part in this. Even if it's just to try and frame you. How could I have cared for someone like that? I feel so dumb that I didn't see this side of him."

Kostas wraps his arms around me tight.

"You couldn't have known this side of him. He was only showing you what he wanted you to see. I'll bet that he never would've shown you this side of him. None of this is on you," he whispers to me.

I hold him tighter and breathe him in. Most days, I can't believe I found my mate. That I get to have what my parents have. Although I'd like to think I would've chosen Kostas even if we weren't fated. He's got such a good heart and he loves his family something fierce. He's my perfect match in every aspect, and we see the world the same way. And his tiger loves my bear, I couldn't ask for more. Well, maybe I can. I want him to be my husband and I want to have cubs with him. Then I will have everything I've ever dreamed of. This Saturday we begin that life, even with everything that's going on, we considered postponing. But this will be the one bright spot in everything that's going on.

Kostas

We got our fight schedules today. I have one fight before we get married on Saturday.

"I got my schedule for this month," I say to Artemis. "Guess who I'm fighting on Thursday."

She sighs softly. "Aion."

I nod and hold her tighter. Of all the fucking weeks to fight him. This is the week.

"Well good. He needs to learn he can't do this to you. To us. Make sure you kick his ass."

I chuckle and kiss her head, I love how feisty she can be.

"I will, Marshmallow. I will."

I will teach Aion that just because he's a bear doesn't mean he's better than me. I only wish we could fight in our animal forms. For some reason that asswipe thinks that because he's a bear, he's a better fighter. Fuck that. My tiger will rip him to shreds.

"When I met the Bastianinis, I found friends in both sets of twins—basically a second family. Because we lived so far away, we couldn't always hang out. They came for vacations and we visited them here too, but that was only once a year, if that.

Then I went through that whole thing with Aion and Daphne. And I thought fuck this. I don't need anyone. That men sucked donkey balls and best friends are worthless. It's crazy how in just an instant, everything can change. Moving here to Chicago, I have the Bastianinis, and now the Mancinis too. But the best part? I found you."

I kiss her, my tongue demanding for her to let me in. She's purring and it makes me instantly hard. But I have to remember there's other people around. Fuck.

Chapter Fourteen

Kostas

Our home is finally done and we're moving in this weekend, right after we get married. Married. Holy shit, I'm finally marrying my mate. My tiger hasn't stopped purring since we chose this Saturday to get married. Two more days.

Today is the fight against Aion. The anger I feel for him has got my adrenaline flowing.

"Don't let him get to you, baby. He likes to talk shit, he used to do that with my brothers when they would spar," Artemis says as she's wrapping my hands.

I kiss her. "I'll do my best, I promise."

I hope I can keep it. Aion knows exactly what buttons to push with me. I just need to keep it together and fight. He's a sore loser, and he did this to himself.,The crowd is pumped for our fight, as we have both started to make a name for ourselves in the SMMA world. As I listen to the fight before us going on, I use the time to stretch. And try to relax a little.

"You're gonna be awesome out there." Artemis smiles at me.

"Only because I know you're waiting for me when I'm done."

I can see the blush coloring her cheeks, and I love it.

"Alright Kostas, you're up next," my dad says as he comes into the room.

"Okay, Dad."

Artemis comes over and kisses me. "Remember, don't let him running his mouth get to you. You're better than him."

I kiss her back. "Don't worry. I got this."

Artemis leaves with my dad to find their seats. It's always way too quiet right before I head out to the ring. It's time. I hear them announce Aion and the crowd is cheering. Now it's my turn and it's just as loud.

I run down the tunnel and head into the ring. Aion's already there, smirking at me.

"You know the rules. Let's have a good fight," the referee says.

We both nod at him.

"After I beat your ass, know that Artemis will be in my bed tonight," Aion snarls at me.

"Even if you were to beat me, she'd never come near you again." I laugh.

The bell rings and we circle each other. I've watched Aion fight, so I know his weaknesses. But it's always more fun to draw it out a little. I let him get a few hits in, and even back me into the corner. Then I smile at him and come out swinging. He has no idea what the fuck is going on. Next thing I know the bell rings and I head to my corner. Aion is stumbling to his.

"Holy fuck that was amazing," Eros says to me. "The look on Aion's face when you really started fighting. He thought you were about to go down."

I laugh. "That's the idea. I think this is going to be over soon. I will say I wish he practiced more."

Ares bursts out laughing. "He thinks he has talent that doesn't need improving. Go show him just how much practice he needs."

I nod as the bell rings.

Again, I let Aion land a few kicks and punches.

Then I unleash a series of combos that takes him down. I stand to the side and wait to see if he gets up. He doesn't.

"The winner—Kostas Nikolaidis!" The referee raises my arm as the crowd cheers.

Aion is glaring at me as he stomps out of the ring. Such bad sportsmanship. I've lost fights too—you congratulate the winner and leave. You don't act like a little kid throwing a tantrum.

"He's such a big baby." Georgios laughs from beside me. "Well that was over pretty fast."

I laugh. "Should I have drawn it out more?"

"No. I don't want you bruised for our wedding," Artemis chimes in.

I wrap my arms around her and kiss her.

"My good luck charm."

We head to the lockers so I can grab a shower and we can get going. Tonight we get to walk through our new home. I'm super excited to see it. Then tomorrow we're going furniture shopping. Just the essentials is what Artemis says. But the look in her eye, along with all the other women in our families...I'm a little scared.

I wish we could get to the bottom of these attacks, but we can't seem to catch a break. We haven't been able to get to the scene early enough to be productive. When we do get there, the scent has already faded and we can only track it so far. It's so fucking frustrating.

But we now know it's a pair of shifters. There are two distinct smells, possibly a male and female duo. That makes us more nervous because it's not just one killer now. And they could still be rogues, but we don't really know.

Artemis

I always love watching Kostas fight. And watching him beat Aion was no different than watching him fight other shifters. The only difference is that Aion thinks he can beat anyone, but he's not special. So when he loses, he acts like a little kid and throws a tantrum. He used to do that back in Greece too.

Kostas fights like my brothers—they do their homework and study their opponents' style beforehand. We all go to every fight and watch. Because you never know who you'll be up against next time.

Our home is gorgeous. It's a two story Victorian-style house, with four bedrooms and four bathrooms. We also have a basement, where we'll have our movie room and bar. It'll take some time to fill it with furniture, but that's okay. We have a lifetime to do it.

Today we're getting things for our bedroom, bathroom, living room and kitchen. I'm so excited... and also not. Both families are going shopping and sometimes that can cause issues, like my brothers thinking they have a say in what goes in my house. Wish me luck.

"So we need couches that'll fit all of us, right?" Ares says as we're driving to the furniture store.

"No. I need a couch that will fit me and Kostas. Not me, Kostas and all of you." I sigh.

"That doesn't work for me. You're gonna need a bigger couch."

I swear my brothers think they're going to move in with us. What the fuck? They can build their own damn houses and fill them all with oversized furniture.

"You know you're not moving in, right?" I squint at my brothers.

Blank stares all around.

"But we'll miss you and need to visit you often." Adonis smirks.

"Uh no you will not, and you won't be at my house all the time."

"How can we protect you if we aren't there?" Apollo gives me a sad look. Because he's my twin, we do have a different bond. But this is ridiculous.

"You'll be able to hear me if I need you from Mamá and Dad's house—where you live."

"That's too far. We need to be closer to be effective." Ares squints at me.

"Well it's a good thing I'll have Kostas. He'll protect me."

All four of my brothers look horribly dissatisfied and shake their heads no.

"He's not big enough," Ares, biggest of my brothers at six foot seven, says.

"Kostas is only one inch shorter than you, Ares. That's not a valid reason." I roll my eyes at him.

"Well an inch is quite a lot," he argues, using his fingers to demonstrate.

I sigh dramatically. "Kostas and I will be fine. And besides, what if the yelling isn't because I'm in danger?"

I wait for them to register what I just said. The first one to get it is my mamá, who starts laughing.

Then it dawns on my dad.

"No. What? Just—no. There will be none of that." I can see him frowning in the rearview mirror.

Then it hits my brothers. And that's when it gets loud.

"Why the fuck would you even go there?" snaps Eros.

"Aww. Gross!" That's Ares.

"Well I want grandcubs. So you and Kostas scream all you want." And that's my mamá. I love her.

"Athena! Don't tell her that!" The vein in my dad's forehead looks like it's about to pop.

So much entertainment for the ride to the furniture store. I just sit back and grin.

Furniture shopping wasn't as bad as I thought it would be. Especially after the car ride we had, which is still making me giggle. My brothers ended up getting to pick our couch, but at least they picked a good one. Each section has a recliner and cup holder. Oh! And between each recliner is an armrest big enough to share. I'll admit I do love it. And the bed Kostas and I picked is like lying on a cloud, but with support. I can't wait to use it. Kostas' and my mamá helped me pick out things for the kitchen and bathrooms. Fluffy. Towels.

Because of tradition, we won't be sleeping in our new house till we're married. Luckily that's only one day away. And with everyone's help, we're able to get everything set up for Saturday. It's all so beautiful. And it was going smoothly until my brothers realized that there weren't any beds for them.

"Wait. We need to go back to the store," Eros says, panic clouding his voice.

"Why? What did we forget?" Kostas asks as he looks around.

"Our beds! Where are we supposed to sleep?" Eros frowns at Kostas.

Kostas looks confused.

"Why do you need beds in our house?" he asks my brothers.

"Do you expect us to sleep on the floor?" Apollo replies.

All the parents are snickering at this point. And I have to admit the looks on their faces are making me giggle.

"You have beds at your house." Kostas stares at them. "You're not living here with us."

"Did you not get the memo? Of course we're living here with you. Who else is going to protect our baby sister?"

The best part of this conversation is that my brothers are one hundred percent serious. And Kostas is so confused. Calliope is almost on the floor laughing. I love our families.

While my brothers are arguing with Kostas over the bed situation, my dad gets a phone call and I watch his face go from laughing to serious. That's not good. We quiet down and wait for him to hang up.

"There's been another killing—a woman. Salvatore and Mac are on their way to pick Apollo and Calliope up. Salvatore has a plan to get you near the crime scene. He'll explain when he gets here in about five minutes.

We all head back to our main house to wait for them. It's the waiting that sucks the most, but at least this time we'll be able to get Apollo and Calliope there sooner than later. I just hope they'll be able to find a good scent this time.

Chapter Fifteen

<u>**Apollo**</u>

These killings are making our new lives in Chicago really hard. Having to watch our backs makes shifting harder too. We can't just run free like we used to. Now, it's constantly making sure where everyone is and being on the alert for humans.

The last time Calliope and I went to the crime scene with Salvatore and Mac, we caught a faint scent of shifters. A male and female, but we couldn't tell if they were the killers or not because it had been too long since it happened.

Tonight is different. We'll get to scent early in

the investigation instead of later, after everyone has trampled all over the scene.

"Hey guys, we gotta go now if we wanna be first on the scene," Mac says, sounding like he ran a marathon. "Sal's in the car. We'll call and explain when we can."

Mac chases Calliope and me out the door and into the car.

"Hey you two. Okay, here's the plan. We're going to have you both jump out close to the crime scene. Then you will act like you're just a couple taking a walk in the park. We will have to make it look like we're telling you to leave the area. But I'm hoping that you'll be able to get a scent in the time you're walking towards us. I know you said you can smell better in your animal form, but the attack was in a park. There's going to be a lot of police around very soon."

"It's okay, we can still get a scent in our human form. Maybe later we can come and do it in our animal form?" I ask.

"We'll try to make it work. They've been wanting to clean the scenes up faster so that people don't catch on that it's an animal attack," Mac says.

Calliope and I both nod.

"Okay, here we are. Follow the sidewalk and go into the entrance that says 'MacArthur Park.' Then turn left. Just follow the path and it will lead you to the scene," Salvatore says.

We jump out of the car at the light. I take Calliope's hand and we start walking. I can already detect the faint smell of shifter.

"You smell that?" she whispers.

"I do. Maybe this time we'll get lucky. So when Salvatore or Mac tell us we have to leave, let's see if we can follow the scent away from the attack."

"Okay. That sounds good. But I'll be honest, rogue shifters really scare me. Growing up, we heard so many stories about them and none of them were good."

"Same here. But don't worry, you're safe with me."

Calliope is like another sister to me, and I would protect her from anything.

We walk slowly like we would if we were on a date, just taking a stroll through the park. The smell of shifter is getting stronger. And I'm hoping we can follow it to wherever that shifter is. Then we'll need to contact the Cleaners to come and take care of them.

"There's the crime scene," Calliope says softly.

The police are setting up lights around the perimeter. We're getting closer and see Salvatore and Mac.

"Sorry, you two can't come this way. You'll have to stay behind the caution tape," an officer says.

"What happened?" Calliope asks in a scared voice.

"Oh don't worry, miss. Nothing to be scared about," he replies.

What a fucking liar. Nothing to be scared about? Asshole.

We start to walk around the taped-off area, sniffing discreetly as we walk.

"I can smell two shifters, plus the victim," I whisper to Calliope.

"Me too. But I can't tell if both shifters did the killing or not." She frowns looking up at me.

We keep walking and following the scent. We've walked quite a ways from the crime scene and what we find is a shed. I can hear voices coming from inside, so we sneak around and find a window. Holy fuck.

"I told you not to kill anymore. We're having a fucking cub and you're still killing!" Xenia screams at the shifter with her.

Fucking Xenia. Holy fucking what the fuck. I look at Calliope and she's just staring at me.

"Just cause you're pregnant doesn't mean I'm going to stop killing these fucking stupid humans!"

the rogue yells back. "And what do you care? You're not killing. I am."

"Oh my fucking god. That's not the point, you moron! You said you would stop!"

"You're a bitch. You've been telling everyone that the cub is your ex's. So why the fuck do you care what I do?"

"I only did that so I can get money you dummy. Kostas is stupid and he will stand up and take care of me and the cub."

"Exactly! Then why are you here? Go to him and leave me the fuck alone."

Crouching here, listening to them argue is making me sick. And I can feel Calliope starting to vibrate. I'm not sure why they can't smell us out here, maybe it's the blood on him that's masking our scent. Right as we're about to leave, the most fucked up thing happens. They start having sex. Full-blown, screaming sex. My fucking eyes and ears. Fuck me.

We quietly leave the area and head to the place where Salvatore told us to meet him.

"Holy shit. That was Xenia Makros, she's Kostas' ex," Calliope growls. "She's been telling everyone that it's my brother's baby. Even though we all know it's not."

"Well from what we just heard, she knows it's

not his. The rogue shifter is the father, and he's not stable. I got a look at his eyes and he's definitely a rogue. A new one, but still a rogue. I'm surprised he's functional enough to be with her."

"And she knows he's the killer. What the fuck?"

"I remember when Salvatore said that Aion went to the detective to tell him Kostas had tigers. He said that Aion came in with a woman. Could that woman have been Xenia?" I ask.

Calliope's eyes are wide as she looks up at me. "Do you really think she's the one who told Aion to do that? Is she sleeping with Aion too? Eww. Gross." She makes vomit noises.

I have to admit that is a sickening thought. We finally see Salvatore and Mac pulling up.

"Did you two find anything?" Mac asks.

"We did, but if it's okay, I'd like to wait to tell everyone at the same time. This involves people we know and it's not going to be pretty."

"Of course. We'll be there in like forty minutes," Mac says.

As we drive back home, I can't understand why would someone like Xenia do this? She has a good life, a good family. I just don't get it. I need to text my dad to get the Cleaners here ASAP.

Apollo: Hey dad, we need the Cleaners here ASAP

Zeus: Shit. Okay. Are you on your way back?

Apollo: Yes. About thirty min away

Zeus: Okay, I'll make the call. We're all waiting for you

"So what did you find out?" Artemis pounces on me as soon as we step through the doorway.

"Whoa. Let me get something to drink, please." I laugh.

"I'll get it. You two start talking," Eros says.

We all go and sit in the living room. I let Calliope tell them how we found the scent and followed it to a shed.

"None of you are going to believe what happened." I sigh.

"I still don't believe it and I saw it with my own eyes." Calliope frowns.

"There is a rogue shifter, but he doesn't seem like an older rogue. I think he had a clan up until pretty recently. His eyes still looked normal from what I could see." I pause.

"Okay, we knew that it was probably a rogue. Get to whatever is the worst part of this," Artemis growls.

"Fine. There's a female shifter that was with him. From what the male said, the female isn't part of the killings. But she's there when he does it."

"Oh for fuck's sake, Apollo. Just tell us who it is," Artemis snaps at me.

"You watch that mouth, Artemis Athanasiou," our dad growls at her.

She stays quiet. Smart bear.

"It's Xenia," Calliope tells everyone.

The room gets deadly quiet, I swear if a mouse farted? You'd hear it.

"You're kidding, right?" Panagiotis asks quietly.

Calliope shakes her head no. "I wish I was, Dad. I saw her. And I heard what she said. That she's saying Kostas is the father because she wants money. But it's really this rogue's kid. And I think she's the one that was with Aion when he went to the police station."

"Holy..." we hear Adonis say. "Who does that? And with a killer? Is she that desperate?"

Kostas

"She's a bitch, but I never thought she would do something like this," I say.

Artemis leans on me as I process everything.

"I already knew the cub wasn't mine. I never touched Xenia, we never even shared a kiss. So I was never worried about that. To know that she's with a killer and trying to get others to believe the cub is mine is fucked up."

"I need to call her dad. He needs to come here so we can talk to him. We need to know if he knows," my dad says.

He steps away to make the call to Lazaros Makros. I don't envy my dad and I hope Xenia's family hasn't been protecting her.

"Lazaros will be here within the hour, and the Cleaners too. I didn't tell him what's going on, just that we needed to talk to him. And that he should bring his wife," Dad tells us.

"I'll make some coffee and get some snacks going," my mamá says as she and Athena head into the kitchen.

"You okay?" Artemis turns to me.

"Yeah. I don't know why Xenia would do this."

"It could be as simple as she wants you back. She knows now how good she had it before, and this is her way of trying to get it back."

"The rogue asked her why she was pinning it on Kostas. Xenia told him it was because Kostas was stupid and would do anything for a cub he thinks is his," Calliope answers.

"But she knows that I know it's not mine. So I wouldn't do anything to help her."

"So she's crazy. Maybe that's the bottom line and the only reason," Ares offers.

"Yeah, maybe. It's just fucking gross. She lived in our home. What if she had hurt one of us?" I frown.

"Well they did say she wasn't killing," Calliope says.

"And? Just cause she didn't kill anyone doesn't make her any better than the rogue killer," Artemis responds.

Calliope sighs. "You're right. She's the same. It's just hard to swallow."

Lazaros gets to the house and we're able to talk to him and his wife, Flora. I believe them when they say that they had no idea what Xenia was doing. That they believed her when she said the cub was mine. I understand why they would, they had no reason not to. And I explain to them that if I thought there was any chance that it was mine, I would be there for them both. But I never even kissed her and I was one hundred percent sure nothing ever happened. They still ask for a DNA test and I agree. If that is the only way to put their minds at rest, I'll do it.

Then the Cleaners arrive and we tell them everything we know. Salvatore and Mac agree to take them to the crime scene in a few hours when the clean-up crew is done. And Calliope and I will take them to the shed. The only stipulation is that the Cleaners give the Makros' two choices. Either they turn in their daughter as the killer or they will take her with them and see if they can help her. They agree to let the Cleaners take her. There's no way that a shifter would survive in prison. And this way, maybe she'll be able to come home one day.

After the Cleaners go with Salvatore to the crime scene and we take them to the shed, we make a plan. We are on our way to Xenia first. She has to know where the rogue shifter lives. And even if she doesn't, the Cleaners will get a better scent off of her and the cub and they'll find him. We hope.

Tomorrow we get a break. Then it's back to making sure no one else gets killed.

Chapter Sixteen

Kostas

Today I'm marrying my mate, the one person that was made just for me. I worried that I would never find that person, but I have. Sitting in this room with the men from all the families is loud, but they're all really happy today. I can't wait to see Artemis. We weren't allowed to see each other after the Cleaners and the Makros' left. And after today? I won't ever have to go to sleep alone.

"You sure you're ready to take Artemis on twenty-four seven?" Adonis chuckles.

I smile at him. "I was born ready."

"Then let's get out there so my dad can go get my sister," Adonis slaps me on the back.

I can't stop smiling—my face might actually get stuck like this. I keep fidgeting while we stand at the altar. What is taking so long? I need to see my marshmallow.

Then she's here. Standing at the end of the aisle, facing me and taking my breath away. She walks towards me with her dad and everything around us seems to fade away. It's just me and my marshmallow.

Artemis

There's a knock at the door and my mamá answers it. My dad and brothers come in to escort Calliope and Mamá to their seats. I'm nervous and excited. I love Kostas and today I'll say it, I should've said it to him a long time ago.

"Are you ready, baby?" my dad asks, his eyes shining with unshed tears.

"I am, Baba." I walk to him and hug him tight. "Thank you for being the best dad ever. For showing me what love should look like. How a man should treat the woman he loves, no matter if she's his fated mate or chosen."

"I'm so proud of the woman you've become, Artemis. You're strong and independent and you make me proud to be your dad every single day."

I sniffle. "You're going to make me mess up my makeup."

He chuckles. "I only speak the truth. Okay. Are you ready?"

I nod as we walk out. Then I see him. My mate. He's smiling at me, that gorgeous smile.

"You take care of my little girl. Mate or not, she's still my baby and I will hurt anyone who hurts her," my dad warns quietly.

"I will protect her to my last breath," Kostas says back to him.

He nods and kisses my cheek. "I love you, Artemis."

"I love you, Baba."

I turn to face Kostas and together we face Raziel. He is the chaplain for the Cimaruta MC Chicago and he offered to officiate our wedding. He goes through his speech for us.

"Kostas and Artemis have written their own vows." He nods at Kostas.

"Mine. That is the first thing my tiger thought

when he saw your bear. The second thing he thought was 'marshmallow.' And since then, you've been my marshmallow. I can't imagine life without you and I don't want to. I'm not sure what I did to deserve you as my mate, but I plan to spend eternity with you making sure I deserve you every day. I love you."

I can't help the tears that are falling, but I have to compose myself enough to say my vows.

"My mate. Somehow in the course of the fates separating our souls at birth, they made sure that the path we both took would lead us back to each other. You are the one that makes me feel beautiful on my worst days. The one that has shown me that I'm worth cherishing. I will always be thankful that I found you. Because in our world, finding our fated mate isn't always a possibility. But know this, even if you weren't my fated mate? I still would've chosen to be with you. I love you so much."

"By the power vested in me by the State of Illinois, I now pronounce you husband and wife. You may kiss your bride."

Kostas kisses me like it's our first and last kiss. Everyone cheers.

We party late into the night. But it's finally time to go home, our home where we will spend our lives together.

Kostas carries me over the threshold and upstairs.

"You know that the tradition is just to carry me over the threshold." I laugh.

"I know, but I can't wait to get you upstairs. You like to take your time sometimes, and I need to know if you taste like a marshmallow. It's all my tiger can think about, because of that, it's all I can think about."

I laugh even harder. "Wait, your tiger still thinks I taste like a marshmallow? What if I don't?"

"He'll get over it." He laughs. "But I have a feeling he's going to be happy."

He gently puts me down and I slowly slide down his body. I turn so he can unzip my dress. Then I let it slowly drop to the floor, I hear him take a sharp breath.

"Fuck, you are gorgeous," he whispers as he kisses the back of my neck.

I slowly turn and take his mouth with mine, using my hands to get his shirt and pants off. I get on the bed and watch him stroke himself.

"I need you. Now," I moan.

Kostas

I don't know if Artemis knows how much I've wanted to hear those words. I get on my knees and slowly nibble my way up her thighs. I breathe in her scent and my tiger goes wild. I start to lick her inner thigh, making my way to her clit. The noises she's making are like music to my ears. And she tastes like marshmallows to me, sweet and pillowy. My tiger is very happy. I slowly slide a finger into her as I latch onto her clit, slowly pumping my finger, curving it so I can hit her sweet spot. She's starting to buck against me...

"Oh fuck," she gasps as I suck harder and add another finger.

"Come for me, baby," I growl as I suck harder. I feel her pussy clenching my fingers like a fucking vice.

"Holy shit," she pants as I slowly release her clit. I lick my fingers, making sure she's watching me. Then I make my way up her body, stopping to kiss and nibble every spot I can.

"You do taste like marshmallows," I whisper as I reach her neck. I graze my canines on her neck as I rub my cock on her slit. "Are you ready?"

"I've been ready for you forever," she moans. I see her canines lengthening as I position myself at her entrance.

The moment I slide into her, we both sink our teeth into each other. The mating bite we share makes me forget everything around us. All I see and feel is Artemis. It is pure bliss. I seat myself all the way in her and stay there for a few moments, relishing in the feeling of having her wrapped around my cock.

I pull out slowly, her pussy is so fucking tight, I slide back in and out trying not to come too soon.

"Please fuck me, Kostas," she cries out.

Who am I to deny her anything? I thrust harder as she's gasping under me, babbling incoherently.

"Fuck, I'm going to come, baby. I need you to come with me."

Just as I say that, she brings her face to my shoulder and sinks her canines into me again. My vision explodes, and I feel my canines lengthening as I sink them into her shoulder as we come together.

I'm not sure how long we lie there together, it feels like hours. But it's probably only a few minutes. I'm pretty sure I black out for a bit, too.

"I love you, Kostas," she whispers.

"I love you, Artemis."

I can feel her drifting off as I hold her tight. This is my world. Right here in my arms.

Epilogue

<u>One month later</u>

Artemis

It's been a month since we got married. Today the Cleaners are picking up the rogue shifter and Xenia. Salvatore and Mac have been helping us this week so that the Cleaners can take them without the police looking for them. They will be taken to Cleaners headquarters. As with all rogue killers, even if he can be rehabilitated, he will never be let out of their facility. As for Xenia? Her baby will be raised by her parents and she'll be in the same facility as the rogue. If she tries to leave, she will be brought up on charges from the Chicago Police. Those were her options. I think she chose wisely.

Salvatore and Mac have convinced Detective Reed that it had to have been a wild rogue tiger and until they catch it in the act, there's nothing more they can do. And because we know that the killer is in custody, there should be no more killings.

We did find out that he wasn't connected to the killings from a couple of years ago. And as of now, we don't know who's responsible. It very well could've been a wild animal.

Aion is still in Chicago with his family. And he still tries to get me to listen to his excuses, even though Kostas and I are married. Aion was forced to marry Daphne when the DNA test for the baby came back and proved it was his cub. Like we all knew it would be. He's such an asshole, and Daphne has been trying to get me to talk to her. I have zero interest in being anywhere near her, let alone talk to her.

Being married to Kostas has been like living the ultimate dream. Sure, we know things won't always be like this, there's going to be times when we have problems. But it's okay, we'll always find a way to get through it.

Kostas

Being married to Artemis has been the best month of my life. Sure it's only been a month, but so far, it's been the best month of my life. We've decided to let fate decide when we have cubs. Which means we just have sex and fuck worrying about protection is the way Artemis puts it. I wholeheartedly agree.

Her brothers weren't kidding, they're at our house more and more lately. And I'm not sure if I like it. They even bought their own damn beds. I mean, come on! They should be at their parents' house. With them here, my siblings have started to stay over too. It's like having six overgrown children living with us.

Artemis and I are still fighting with the SMMA every week, she said she'll take a break when she gets pregnant. Now I love watching my wife kick ass, but the idea of her being pregnant? Holy fuck, yes.

"Do you think Xenia will learn her lesson and be released?" Artemis asks me.

I shrug my shoulders. "I'm not sure I want her out in the world. She's good at pretending, and manipulating. I just hope their people can see through her lies."

"I feel so sad for her cub. It's not the baby's fault that she's a psycho and their dad is crazy." She frowns. "Maybe he can still be rehabilitated."

I wrap my arms around her, I love her compassion for this cub even after all the shit that's happened.

"Xenia's parents are good people. I'm sure that however it plays out, the cub will be raised right."

Artemis sighs and turns to look at me. "I hope we raise our cubs right."

"Of course we will."

"Are you sure? Because we can't return them if it's too hard."

I chuckle. "I would never want to return our cubs."

"Good to know," she says as she hands me a piece of paper.

I read it, then read it again. I'm pretty sure it says she's pregnant.

"Holy shit. Is this real?" I blurt out.

Artemis laughs. "Of course it's real. The doctor says I'm only three weeks along. So it's really early to tell anyone. But I was feeling yucky and I was already two weeks late. So I decided to go and see."

I pick up my wife and kiss her. "You keep making me happier and happier."

About the Author

Hi! I'm Natalie. I published my first book, Aftermath in August 2021. I've been lucky enough to find my own insta-love-at-first-sight person. We have a daughter who drives us crazy and a corgi who adds to the chaos. I love hockey (Chicago Blackhawks), MotoGP (Motorcycle Racing), and baseball (Chicago Cubs). When I'm not writing, you can find me studying or crafting. Or crafting when I should be studying.

Nataliearthurbooks.com

Giovanna

Everything I thought about my life was a lie and because of that, trust became non-existent for me. Then I met Declan. He pushed his way into my life, determined to prove to me that not everyone is a liar. He's a hockey player and we all know the reputation of hockey players. But I want to trust someone again...maybe he's the one?

<u>Declan</u>

Hockey has been my focus for as long as I can remember. The day I met Giovanna, my life changed. Hockey would always be my first love. But she would be my last. Something happened to her and she's afraid to trust me. But that's okay, I'll show her that I'm real. That we're real.

Aftermath is the first book in my Mancini Legacy Series. All books are standalone, but it's best if read in order. There is mention of characters from my Cimaruta MC Chicago Series.

https://books2read.com/Aftermath-ManciniLegacy

Sebastiano

I had given up on meeting my person, content to be the protector of my family. Then one day I met her. But someone else was laying claim to her. If she was happy, I would step back and watch her from afar. But then I saw the marks on her and I knew I needed to save her.

Schuyler

It seems like I've been struggling most of my life. Just my

sister and me against the world. Then I thought I met the man of my dreams. Turns out he's the man from my nightmares. I can't run and I can't escape from him. Then I met Sebastiano. He made me feel safe from the moment he took my hand in his. He says I will be his, but he doesn't know about the monster that's in my life. The one that won't let go.

Saving Her is the second book in my Mancini Legacy Series. All books are standalone, but it's best if read in order. There is mention of characters from my Cimaruta MC Chicago Series.

https://books2read.com/SavingHer-ManciniLegacy

<u>Luciana</u>

Women on an MC council? It's unheard of until now.
Love at first sight? That's a new one for me too. I was
convinced I didn't need someone to make me happy.

Then I slammed into Rónán.

Literally.

In an instant, he turned my world upside down. But can
he handle the MC life?

<u>**Rónán**</u>

My life was going the way I planned it. Then the most beautiful woman stepped into my path and changed my life forever. I know she's keeping things from me. And that's okay...for now.

Because she's mine.

She just doesn't know it yet.

Choices is the first book in my Cimaruta MC Chicago Series. All books are standalone, but it's best if read in order. There is mention of characters from my Mancini Legacy Series.

https://books2read.com/Choices-CimarutaMCChicago

Francesco

I met the love of my life at fourteen. She had my heart the moment I saw her. But when you're young and stupid you don't always make the right decisions. That's what happened to me. I let the temptations of my job distract me from the one thing I couldn't live without. I had lost all hope, but fate gave me another chance. I have to make it up to her. I know she's hiding something from me. Will she let me in and give me a second chance?

<u>**Maeve**</u>

I thought I had it all. Sure I may have been young, but when it's real, you just know. That was, until he ended things. I never saw it coming. Now he's back and he wants another chance. Can I really trust him not to break my heart again? I want to believe him. I've never stopped loving him. But it's not just me I have to protect anymore.

Can they find their way back to the happily ever after they were meant to have? Or will they be pulled apart again, shattering all hope?

Reclaiming Our Forever is the second book in my Cimaruta MC Chicago Series. All books are standalone, but it's best if read in order. There is mention of characters from my Mancini Legacy Series.

https://books2read.com/ReclaimingOurForever-CimarutaMCChicago

<u>Amante</u>

Relationship? No.

Love? Hell no.

Forever? Never.

A quick hook up and that was that. I had my family and my club and that's all I needed. Until the day she walked in. With her I wanted more than one night, but when I got out of the shower she was gone. But I will find her. Then I'll just have to convince her we belong together.

<u>Charmaine</u>

Love is nothing but a lie. I watched my parents crash and burn and nothing and no one could change my mind. Until him. My tattooed, hunky biker man. Wait, did I say mine? That can't happen. But he says all the right things, and makes me feel like I'm the most special girl in the world. Can we make it work?

Notch the Plan is part of the Notchin' Boots Series. There is mention of characters from my Mancini Legacy Series and my Cimaruta MC Chicago Series.

https://books2read.com/NotchThePlan-NotchinBoots

<u>Hollis</u>

The people you're born to don't always turn out to be your 'family'. Families can be chosen, and I chose the Cimaruta MC. They've been there with me for the last six years, and I thought I had everything I needed. One night was all it took to make me want more. But she's hiding something from me and I need to know what it is. I will save her from anything. That much I do know.

<u>Lila</u>

My life was finally going smoothly. It was me and my daughter against the world. I worked at a club called Club Curve—I'm a curvy girl, so why not? Then one night, HE walked in. Now he's turning my life upside down and I'm not sure how to feel about it. My biggest fear is about to become a reality.

Just as you are is a stand alone and part of the Club Curve series. But there is mention of characters from my Mancini Legacy and Cimaruta MC Chicago series.

https://books2read.com/JustAsYouAre-ClubCurve

Aiden

Motorcycle racing has been my life since I could walk and talk. It was all I ever needed. Or so I thought. Then I met the one woman that made me want more. One day, the unthinkable happens—a racing accident causes me to lose all my memories of her. But I still feel her in my soul, even if my brain can't remember her.

Élodie

I wanted a knight in shining armor, but what I got was a wolf in disguise. After escaping from him, I met a man willing to give me everything I ever wanted. Then in a split second, he was taken from me. Not physically, but mentally. The man I love doesn't remember who I am, but I'm determined to get him back.

Racing Back to Love is part of the Forget-Me-Not Series. There is mention of characters from my Mancini Legacy Series.

https://books2read.com/RacingBackToLove-ForgetMeNot

www.ingramcontent.com/pod-product-compliance
Lightning Source LLC
Chambersburg PA
CBHW061528310726
48972CB00008B/2362